APPROVAL

A NOVEL BY: *John D. Rutter*

Saraband ⊚

Published by Saraband,
Salford Quays and Glasgow

www.saraband.net

ISBN: 9781913393120

Printed and bound in Great Britain by Clays Ltd, Elcograf S.p.A.

10 9 8 7 6 5 4 3 2 1

This is a work of fiction.
All characters are a product of the author's imagination.

"John Rutter's *Approval* is many things at once. A powerful meditation on judgement. A transfixing fable of a Kafka-esque application process. A complex tragedy about fatherhood. But it's also a simple, affecting and beautifully wrought story of one couple's journey towards what they most desire – a child – and the cost of reaching out for one. A hugely promising debut." RODGE GLASS

"An accessible and relatable tale of domestic heartache… It has a warmth and intimacy to it." ABI HYNES on 'Motivation', *The Short Story*

"Rutter gives us a skilled, melancholy view of a troubled relationship." ANDRE VAN LOON on 'Green Gables', Litro.co.uk

"The beauty of this story is its understatement; what is left unsaid mirrors precisely the relationship's downfall. It works through the small powerful details." SARAH SCHOFIELD on 'Green Gables', *The New Short Review*

"There are some lines which really capture the bitterness of relationships gone wrong, highlighting Rutter's ability to pinpoint emotional truths succinctly." SARAH DOBBS on 'My Knee', *The Short Story*

"[An] essential, Tardis-quality … there's far more inside than the outside, apparently, could possibly contain." EMMA DARWIN on 'David's Thing' *Words With Jam*

"Fun to mull over as a piece of pure fiction, but the real-world correlates ⌐ ⌐ ⌐ ⌐ ⌐ ⌐ ⌐ ⌐ ⌐ DEN O'REILLY o

"John D Ru ⌐ ⌐ ⌐ ⌐ ; in everyday li

Contents

For Lin

Judgement does not come suddenly;
the proceedings gradually merge into the judgement.

Franz Kafka, *The Trial*
(Originally published in German as *Der Process,* 1925)

Welcome to the
Prospective Adopters Workbook

This workbook is designed to help you through the journey towards adoption. It will give you a chance to think about the benefits and challenges you will face and will help you to decide whether adoption is right for you and whether this is the right time to set off along this path.

In accordance with the Statutory Guidelines, Stage 1 of the assessment procedure should take no more than two months and Stage 2 should take approximately four months, unless there are unforeseen delays such as, for example, late references. It is anticipated that 25–30 pages are required to complete the workbook. This will then lead to the Prospective Adopter's Report (PAR). You should talk to your family, friends and support network and refer to the materials you will have been provided with on your three-day Fostering and Adoption Training and Development Programme. This will help you on the journey through assessment, then to panel and approval and, ultimately, to matching.

You will be expected to review your personal history, including any experience of parenting, previous relationships, your work history, previous addresses, references, personal finances and medical history.

You will also be subject to statutory criminal record checks (DBS – Disclosure and Barring Service, formerly known as CRB).

It is important that you are completely truthful as any discrepancies with your references may cause delays to the process. Your allocated social worker will check all of the details and will use them as the starting point for their discussions with you. This is a two-way process, so that the adoption service can learn all about you and what makes you tick, and exercise proper scrutiny, so that we can ensure that any child will be appropriately matched and safe in your care.

Your Journey
Towards Fostering and Adoption
through Collaboration

Registration

|

Meet and Greet

|

Assessment Stage 1
Initial Checks

|

Assessment Stage 2
Full Assessment
and Training

|

**Approval and
Matching**

1.0 Motivation for Adoption

Part 1 is all about exploring why you think you would be a good parent. Are you a parent of older children already and want to extend your family, or will this be the first child in your household?

Your social worker will be keen to understand your motivation to adopt, your pathway to the decision to apply and your present circumstances, including whether you have or have had any children or stepchildren together or separately (if applying as a couple).

If you have attempted to have your own biological child, including IVF or any other fertility treatment, you must describe where you are up to in that process and your past experiences (e.g. any failed pregnancies).

It is not allowed for an application for adoption to proceed concurrently with any fertility treatment such as a private IVF programme. If there is any risk of pregnancy during the approval process, you must discuss this with your social worker before you proceed, and you will be expected to take precautions.

Motivation

A couple are standing in the doorway of a small bedroom. His arms blanket her from behind. A beech IKEA table sits in one corner. A die cutting machine is buried under stacks of card in pastel shades, hand-made miniature flowers and a clutter of dies and tools. There is an unassembled wooden cot beneath the window. Otherwise the room is unfurnished. A fan of paint sample swatches lies in the centre of the beige carpet. The walls are magnolia.

'Are are we settled on Winnie the Pooh?' David asks.

'Okay. Paint the walls yellow.'

'Honey Mustard.'

'Honey Mustard. Then I will add some details and stickers.'

'Shall we do it this weekend?'

'No, let's wait till we know for definite.'

Cici strokes her flat stomach. She turns round to face him. 'You agree with Scarlett?' she asks.

'All right. And Eric for a boy?' He grins.

She shakes her head and puts her hand on his chest. 'We're not naming our baby after a comedian or a footballer. Go and enjoy yourself. I'm going to rest.'

'Are you sure you don't mind?'

'Behave yourself. No smoking. And find out how Dougie's little ones are.'

'I will.'

He kisses her on the forehead and leaves her looking at the empty room.

* * *

Two middle-aged men are leaning across a circular pub table. One is tall with salt and pepper hair. The other is thick-set and unshaven; his chest is wide, so the top three buttons of his checked shirt are undone. There is a milk stain on his shoulder.

'How was your visit to the IVF clinic?' Dougie, the broader man, asks.

'I kid you not,' David says. 'Private *murders* the NHS. You'd have loved this place.'

Dougie chuckles.

'Huge La-Z-Boy leather armchair, forty-inch flat-screen telly with remote...' David makes a 'fish-was-this-big' gesture with both hands, then takes a swig of beer. 'The video menu was, I must say, extensive. Plenty of motivation.'

'Literally.'

'Don't use that word, Dougie.'

'Tell me more.'

'Imagine a comprehensive library accommodating every taste and proclivity...'

'Every taste, like? Literally?'

'They might not delve as deep as the darkest recesses of your twisted Geordie mind, but there was plenty to pick from.'

'And may one ask what you chose from this smorgasbord of viewing delight?'

'That's private.'

Dougie scratches his stubble. 'So, I gather this was a more successful, erm, production, than last year with the NHS?'

'I'm still trying to get the whole cupboard trauma out of my mind.'

'I'm sure you're exaggerating.'

'I'm telling you. It was a broom cupboard on the main corridor of the hospital with a chair and a box of tissues. Not even a magazine – not allowed. I could hear a group of people outside the door discussing their NHS pensions. And everyone knows I'm in there!'

'You're doing Jeff Goldblum hands again.'

'First time was even worse. We were still trying to keep it a secret then.' David leans in and glances from side to side. 'Did I tell you about Cici's colleague?'

'At the IVF clinic?'

'We're sitting there on egg and sperm day – this was the *first* time – and this couple walks in. Turns out he's an engineer at her place, rugby-type.'

Dougie folds his arms. 'Awkward.'

'The women went off with the nurses. Me and him sat waiting our turn, talking about football.'

'They've only got one room?'

'I said, "After you, mate," and sat there waiting while he did what he needed to do.'

'And what were you thinking?'

'I was thinking I should have gone first, like a penalty shoot-out. He was only in there five minutes, hadn't even broken sweat. He was a big lad, too, half my age.'

'Pressure.'

'Thankfully he didn't shake hands. Then it was my turn. Took ages, couldn't concentrate. No wonder it didn't work out.' He watches the dregs slide down the inside of his glass.

Dougie shuffles in his seat. 'You mustn't blame yourself.'

'They did say my numbers are a bit low, you know, owing to me being a bit older these days.'

'You are knocking on a bit.'

'Thanks. I'm still scoring at over thirty million a pop though.'

'Aye, plenty there. And is this the last go?'

'Cici was a mess last time. She never lets on, but I could tell she'd been crying when I got home. We've agreed no more after this. Five years is enough.'

'Let's hope you hit the jackpot this time. Third time lucky, eh?' He softly chinks his glass against David's.

'I can't let her go through all that again.' David stares at his empty glass. He thinks of Cici drinking from a plastic hospital cup. Images of hospitals are never far from his mind. 'Must be my round.'

'Always.'

David gazes at the decor while the barmaid pulls two pints of Cumberland. The Cock and Bull has been David and Dougie's regular haunt for so long they don't even arrange to meet. They just turn up every Friday after work. His eyes scan walls decorated with black and white photos of buses and trucks, musical posters from a bygone era. There's an upright piano and a parade of guest beers.

Dougie is ready with more questions as David carefully places two full pints on stained real ale beer mats.

'Tell us a bit more about this private clinic.'

'You don't want a blow by blow...'

'Don't be a wazzock, you kna' what I mean.'

'Same as NHS really, but you have to take a credit card with you.'

'How much is it?'

'Six grand so far.'

'They can afford proper facilities then. So what happens?'

'Cici has injections for thirty days to stop her cycle, then another month when she carries on with them *and* another lot to speed up production, and no sex at all.' He takes a gulp of beer as images force themselves into his mind of Cici drawing drugs from a miniature glass vial and injecting herself in the belly. 'Then I've got to produce half a cupful on demand.'

'No wonder they make the environment as encouraging as possible.'

'Then they take some eggs out and I, erm, do my bit, and they put the two together.'

'Very well explained, doctor. Perhaps best you didn't follow the medical career, eh? And how big is the… receptacle?' Dougie lifts his glass.

'It's only small. You've got to be accurate.'

Dougie shakes with silent laughter. 'Where's she while this is taking place?'

'She's under anaesthetic, having the eggs taken out.' David's eyes wander to an overweight yellow Labrador snoozing in the corner. His mind drifts to Cici's sleeping face; she doesn't have her usual half-frown of pain when she's asleep. He turns back to his friend. 'The consultant's a professor-type, charming man. Told us an analogy about egg warehouses and sperm factories. Few minutes later, Cici's counting down from ten like she's pissed, and the nurse does this as my cue.' David curls his finger.

'Didn't you ask her if she'd give you a hand?'

David shakes his head. 'I'm happy with Cici.'

'Aye, she's a belter that one.' His face becomes serious. 'What happens next?'

'They have this thing called ICSI.'

'What's that?'

'They take an individual sperm – one of the strongest-looking ones – and insert it directly into the egg. They do a few to increase the chances.'

'How do they choose which ones?'

'They go for the ones that are swimming straightest. Not that there's anything wrong with my boys.'

'Course not, just a few pissed ones.'

'Exactly. Then they monitor the embryos on this new gadget they've got and after a few days they call us and put them back in.'

'Again, excellent technical explanation.'

'We've agreed if this one fails we'll look at adoption.'

Dougie frowns. 'I saw something on the Internet. There's money in this year's Budget for adoption. That and a penny on ale.' He softly pats his glass.

'Do you ever get any actual work done at that place since I left?' David asks.

'Not as such, but they don't seem to mind.'

'I heard something about them speeding up the approval process.'

'Not a surprise with this council.' Dougie shakes his head.

'That's what I'm worried about.' David leans forward. 'Did I tell you I enquired about fostering once?'

'Howay, man.'

'After I split up with Danny's mum.'

'How is the little fella?'

'Not so little, these days. Still plays a lot of football.' David remembers a race for a ball, wrestling on a wet lawn, being pinned down and flicked on the forehead.

'You were saying about fostering…' Dougie prompts.

'Yeah, they were advertising on the radio. It had all that equal opportunities stuff. You know, "regardless of marital status…"'

'I can see you doing that.'

'They sent this young social worker along. She took one look at my suit and the piano. I got a rejection letter two weeks later.'

'Harsh.'

'They never even let me fill in the application. Turns out they only want the kind of single man that lives with a woman.'

'Or another man.' Dougie glances around the pub. 'Are you forced to go to the council for adoption? I wouldn't fancy all the investigations they do.'

'Not with your murky past. You are if you want a baby, and Cici's set on a baby, especially after all she's been through.' David looks at the dog again.

'Aye,' Dougie says. 'Toddlers is the best part. But don't you get damaged kids, like?'

'As long as they don't have something really serious you manage, don't you?'

'Same as your own really; or like you with Danny.'

'How are your monsters? Cici was asking.'

'Horrible as ever, tearing the house apart. McTiny always asks when he's going to the park with Cici.'

'Buy one off you?'

'It's very tempting, lad, but get yer fuckin' own. They are monsters but they're our bairns.' Dougie pulls back his frayed cuff, exposing a scratched watch. 'I'm off after this one; check they're tucked in proper.'

'Me too, get back to Cici.'

* * *

Cici is lying on her back with her legs in stirrups beneath a humming air-conditioning unit. She is wearing only a loose blue hospital gown, no underwear. She is straining her head to see a monitor above her. At her side a nurse is rolling a scanner over the flat stomach of her patient and asking her to confirm her name and date of birth for the third time while giving gentle reassurance with her eyes. Two doctors in white coats are whispering below the monitor. The male one has a strong Eastern European accent.

In the corner of the room, perched on a flimsy plastic chair, sits David. He is bent forward, arms on legs, fingers intertwined. He looks up at the sound of Cici's name.

A square hatch in the opposite wall opens. A face appears, a young woman with blue eyes, metal-framed glasses, a white coat and a mask. She asks the doctors whether they are ready. They speak softly and make small head movements that can only mean 'no'. They return to their secret debate.

The hatch clicks shut.

David stares at Cici until she twists her head round. He sticks his tongue out. She tries to smile, fails. Her brown eyes are glistening. He looks at two information sheets on the wall beside him. Photos of mothers holding babies next to men with good teeth in woolly jumpers; statistics in cheerful yellow; a graph, '40% success rate'; images of splitting cells – two, four, eight; perfect embryos; photogenic babies.

The double doors swing open. A man with tufty white hair and a pink tie strides through, causing everyone (except Cici, in stirrups) to hold themselves more upright. He grins confidently at the patient and stands very close to the two doctors. His crisp, plummy voice is clearer than the others but not loud enough that any words can be heard. He frowns at the monitor.

The woman doctor lowers her head and points out a detail on the paper in her hand.

Pink Tie turns round with a professional smile. 'My colleagues are concerned at this quite large shadow near the ovary. Fluid, perhaps.' He points his hand as if delivering a lecture. 'Given that we were so pleased with the embryos, I think it best if we pop the pair of them back in the fridge for now. They'll be safe there for a few months. We'd better deal with this shadow first…'

Pink Tie carries on speaking. He's explaining medical terms and telling them there is a choice of strategies.

David and Cici don't say anything. He is bent over again. She is trying to avoid eye contact, but eventually she looks up. She is sobbing silently, holding her lips together to prevent a scream. Her face is soaked.

His throat is blocked. He closes his eyes.

Can't breathe drowning school swimming pool chlorine in my eyes boy drowned here emergency ambulance can't look Cici hurting no baby hospital waiting injections scars no parking spaces dead babies Cici bleeding sperm in a plastic cup shadow lump cancer operation change for the car park perfect embryos dead twins blood on the bathroom floor Cici crying last chance boys don't cry can't breathe...

The nurse touches his shoulder. 'Are you all right?'

'Mm? We'll be fine, I'll look after her.' He takes a clean tissue from his jacket pocket and moves to Cici's side.

The nurse heads for the door. 'I'll leave you alone while she gets dressed, and I'll take your invoice through to reception. You can stay here a few minutes if you want a bit of privacy.' She smiles at Pink Tie. 'Professor Knight will write to your GP about the next steps.'

'Thank you very much.'

2.0 Family Tree

Insert a diagram showing your main family relationships: parents, grandparents, children (including stepchildren and adopted children), siblings and all marriages (current and former). Include dates of birth (and death, if applicable). Complete one family tree each if applying as a couple.

If you have any difficulties with reading or writing – such as dyslexia – the Council will provide you with full support. Translations of this document and all of the training materials, policies and procedures are available in Punjabi, Hindi, Gujurati, Urdu and Polish.

Family Tree: David Potter

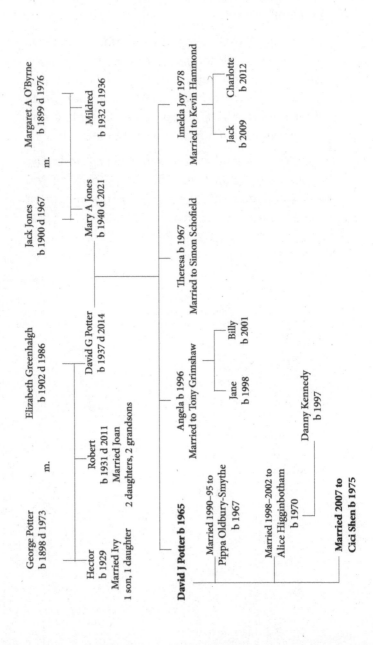

2.1 Family Relationships

Describe the key relationships in your family tree. Think about the dynamics of your own family. What were your relationships with your own parents like? How did their relationship work and how did your parents help your emotional development? How has your relationship with your parents evolved during your life? If your parents are now elderly, how has that changed your relationships and how do you feel about them? If you are adopted yourself, please explain how that has affected your understanding of parental relationships.

If you have siblings, how has your relationship with them developed and evolved over the years? Have you ever experienced any sibling rivalry or jealousy? How do you think that has affected your own attitudes towards parenting, especially if you are considering adopting a sibling group?

If you have children of your own, including adopted children or stepchildren, explain how you intend to manage the impact they may have on any potential adopted child and how you anticipate the dynamics of your family will change.

Opposite Sides

At the back of a 1930s semi-detached suburban house an internal wall divides two rooms. The wall has been there for forty-five years; this part of the house is an extension. The couple, presently on opposite sides of the wall, have lived here for sixty years, twenty-five alone after the last of their children left.

On the right is a long lounge. It has a blue carpet with a faux William Morris design of cream-and-blue flowers. At one end of the room sits a glass-covered, green, wooden dining table inlaid with images of Chinese stories and surrounded by six matching green chairs. A dark wood-effect sideboard is cluttered with a gaggle of graduation pictures – some in wooden frames, several in silver, two in gold. By the window rests a single hospital bed with side rails; the sheets have been removed and the window is ajar, even though it is raining; the pink and cream *fleur-de-lis*-patterned curtains are frayed. Next to the bed is a chunky, burgundy-coloured, motorised tilt-and-recline chair. Directly in front of the chair is a huge old-style CRT television; on the TV a man and woman are nodding and grinning on a chat show, which blares out at maximum volume.

In the chair an old woman is slumped motionless, surrounded by several pillows, a child's blanket covering most of her, the control for the chair clutched in her right hand, which trembles insistently. She has the look of a large balloon that has had half of the air let out. There are only a few tufts of hair on the porcelain-grey skin half-covering her skull.

On the left of the wall is the kitchen. Every marble-effect worktop is piled high with stacks of mail, scraps of note paper and assorted jars and bowls filled with buttons, pens, broken clothes pegs, copper coins, coloured elastic bands and Lego bricks. There is a cream Roberts radio with dust caked over the dials; *Bye Bye Baby* is playing on Radio 2. There are rectangular cupboards, with peeling brown laminate finish, fixed to the walls, and four burners on the hob with decades of burnt grease and two filthy saucepans. The oak-effect lino has several bare patches where it has worn right through, and it curls up by the back door.

An old man is hunched at the kitchen table with his back to the lounge wall. On the table sits a hand-written 'to do' list, a mustard-coloured retractable pencil, several faded Lake District coasters and an assortment of bottles of tablets. His wears a lop-sided droopy smile. He is squinting at the front page of the *Warrington Guardian*.

On the other side of the wall, she begins to yell, 'Love? Love...' The only name they use for each other; never their actual names, not 'Mum' or 'Dad' for decades now.

He doesn't move.

She shouts, 'Are you putting the kettle on? I'm parched. It must be time for my elevenses.'

He turns the page of the newspaper. When the square plastic wall clock reaches exactly eleven, he pushes himself to his feet and clicks on the kettle.

She shouts again, louder this time.

He fiddles with the single damp sheet draped over a flimsy airer, takes a faded Silver Jubilee milk jug out of the fridge, and sniffs the milk.

'Can you hear me? You can't hear me, can you? I'm stuck...'

He puts two cups and saucers, a tablet from each of three different bottles, two tea-spoons and a packet of pink and yellow squared cake on a worn wooden tray.

'It's hopeless; I can't carry on like this... I need you where I can see you. Can you hear me?' she sobs. 'I don't think I can carry on.'

While the kettle rumbles, he reads a hand-written letter on a lined A4 sheet, holding it at arm's length. The top line says, *To whom it may concern.* He adds a note with his retractable pencil.

'Help... Help... Somebody help me! Nobody can hear me. Where's the phone?'

He stares into the damp garden. The wet grass is overgrown. A group of pigeons squabbles over a few bread crusts.

'Help! I can't cope. Somebody help me!'

He makes the tea with a series of automatic movements and brings the tray into the lounge.

'Why didn't you answer?' she pleads. 'I can't move. You know I need you to be here in case I need anything... I need to move; my sores are getting worse. Oh no! You've forgotten the knife. You know you need a knife with Battenberg... Always forgetting things, these days. Did you let it brew? You never leave it long enough...'

He pours the tea and clears his throat. 'I've written another letter to the boss man at the council,' he announces. 'I've told 'em the perishing lot of 'em should be sacked. I didn't agree to the so-called care plan, sending care workers in at all hours. I'm not having all and sundry traipsing though the house. I can manage perfectly well without that crowd interfering, thank you very much!'

'Don't put it there, love, I can't reach. I haven't got a tissue... Can you get me some tissues when you go to get the knife? And when you go to Morrisons on Friday, get some more of those aloe vera tissues, not the ones you got last time, they're the wrong ones. Put it on the list. And I need some more of that cream for my skin; take the packet so you get the right one, don't get that cheap one; and can you close the window now and pass me the other blanket? I'm cold. I need to move my shoulder, I can't reach... Turn the telly down a bit...'

He roughly moves her pillows around and continues, 'I've told 'em. If those stupid women think they can order me round, they've got another think coming. It all started with that trainee girl, the Indian one. Absolutely clueless…'

'Why don't you wear your hearing aid? What if I need something? What if something happened? I mean, anything could happen… Don't forget the tissues, will you? And you need to empty the bin… Have you put the recycling out?'

The door-bell rings. Neither of them hears. A Nokia phone vibrates on the kitchen table.

* * *

The bright lights have come on in the kitchen. Four middle-aged siblings are sitting around the table, all wearing dark colours. The cracked mugs they are drinking from are the same ones they used when they all lived here a lifetime ago.

'We should knock down the wall between the kitchen and the lounge,' David, the only male, says, pointing at the partition wall.

'That's not what Dad would have wanted.' Theresa speaks exactly as a schoolteacher would to a naughty five-year-old.

'Ner-ner-ner-ner,' David replies, in the voice of a naughty five-year-old. 'That's the whole point! He had no idea what he was doing, even before he went mad.'

Theresa sighs. 'He didn't go mad; he had dementia. And we need to get to the point. We can't leave the kids with Kevin all day.'

David takes a deep breath. 'Look, if we take down the wall between here and the lounge, it will create a big L-shaped open space, like Joy's house. No one wants a house where you have to go along a corridor and through a couple of doors to get from the kitchen to the living room. It's all about open-plan, these days.'

'I'd rather we just got rid of the bloody house.' Angie slurps her tea. 'Now they've finally gone, I'd prefer to take my share and move on. They dragged it out long enough. I don't care if we'd get a few thousand more each.'

Theresa purses her lips and sniffs. She has never treated Angie as her older sister. 'It's got more to do with Dad's heritage and what he would have wanted.'

'What he wanted was to tell everyone what to do the whole time and he'd batter them if he didn't get his way. It was like that when we were growing up, and it was the same when he ranted at Mum's care workers.' Angie reaches for the tea-pot, which has a chipped spout and is wearing a home-made woollen cosy whose pattern is long covered by stains. 'And this is the first thing going on the skip.'

'I'm sure you're exaggerating, and besides that's all irrelevant now,' Theresa says. 'We all voted that we'd do the house up. If we do, it might be worth nearer to four hundred.'

Joy joins in. 'Well, I'm the only one with a mortgage, so I'd rather we got the most out of it, but can we pleeease stop arguing.'

The conversation continues in a circular motion for a further ten minutes before shifting to an argument over who will sort out Mum's books. Theresa, having published an article in *Mechanical Engineering News*, was lauded by Mum. David's first novel was greeted with, 'That's two authors in the family!' Theresa's graduation picture is the biggest.

'I'll put my name down for the books,' she announces.

David's mind drifts to a night somewhere around 1974 when Dad first built the wall, one of the last parts of the 'The Extension', a three-year project. He must have still been working late in the evening because *Match of the Day* was on and it was one of the first times David was allowed to stay up that late. The extension, built to make room for Joy, had been open-plan, and when the arguments started with the builders because the money ran out,

Dad decided to try his hand at bricklaying and had built the partition wall himself as a single skin out of concrete common bricks. The middle section had been laid unevenly so that, by the top, the wall had a distinct curve, with the bricks lower in the centre creating a sort of lop-sided smile.

'Doesn't matter that,' Dad announced when David noticed that the wall wasn't straight. 'Just as strong – probably stronger, the load will transfer more efficiently, and it's not a supporting wall anyway. No one will see it when I've plastered it.' The wall was left un-plastered for the first several years and had been partially covered with an old green curtain.

Theresa has moved the agenda to the house clearance.

Angie is the first to wade in. 'We should have a bloody great bonfire and burn the lot.'

'There must be some things of value,' Theresa says.

'Yes, there's loads of demand for cheap post-war furniture full of woodworm, and urine-soaked mattresses,' David says.

'Don't be like that, these were Mum and Dad's things,' Theresa says. 'They have sentimental value.'

'Who's got that picture of Dad in his army uniform?' David asks.

'I've got it,' Theresa says. 'I can make copies if necessary.'

'Don't bother.'

Angie is facing a double height cupboard whose door won't close. 'I can't wait to find the treasure in all those Heinz labels and vouchers, and bagsie I get first choice on the pans.'

'I can see everyone's upset. Let's try and focus on the task,' Theresa says.

'There's nothing I want, and these lights are giving me a migraine,' Angie says. 'Does anyone want any of the furniture?'

'Of course not… Have we met?' Joy replies with a grin. 'Have you seen our house?'

'Just 'cos you've got a nice big house by the golf course,' Angie says.

'Angie can have Mum's ejector seat; she'll be getting to that stage soon,' Joy says.

Angie sticks her tongue out.

'And I do *not* want that bloody stupid ugly green "I got a great deal" Chinese dining table, it's horrid,' David adds.

'You have to, you've got a Chinese wife,' Joy says.

'In that case, you've got to have all the crockery for your fancy kitchen, and the free-with-petrol 1970s glasses.'

'Touché.'

Theresa explains in detail how she plans to administer the list she has started. It will be a SharePoint file and everyone can add their names to items.

David takes off his glasses and rubs the sides of his nose. He glances at the industrial strip lights on the ceiling and blinks. Angie is listing items of furniture out loud to disparaging murmurs. Theresa is typing on her Surface Pro.

'Can't we just get one of those house-clearance companies?' David asks. 'We could get Emmaus or one of those charity recycling places.'

Theresa peers over her reading glasses. 'I think we should do things properly.'

Joy joins in. 'I don't think anyone would want any of this stuff. I mean, look at it! They never even let me pay for a cleaner.'

'It all wants to go on a skip, the bloody lot of it,' David says. 'Hoarders, the pair of them. Not a single bloody thing worth keeping in the whole house.'

'Listen, shall we take a bit of a break?' Joy suggests. 'We're not getting anywhere. Let's all have a look around and see if there is any stuff we can take away with us today while we've all got empty cars.'

Approval

'Good idea,' David says, rising to his feet. 'I'll have a rummage in the attic.' His initials had been marked against the attic on Theresa's spreadsheet.

As he leaves the room, all three sisters fiddle with their smartphones.

* * *

David strides through the hall past a metre-tall stack of *Daily Telegraph*s, muttering. 'I'll knock the damned thing down myself. I'll smash it with a fucking sledge-hammer, stupid uneven fucking wall!'

He pauses and glances at the heavy bolt of the front door. When Angie was eighteen, he used to creep down and let her in at night after Dad had locked the door.

He takes the stairs two at a time, grabbing the brand-new handrail on one side and the many-times painted banister on the other. 'Bloody stupid handrails. She couldn't get upstairs even before they fitted them, bloody size of her.'

The top two stairs creak loudly. David makes a noise that might be a small laugh. He steps back down and climbs the last few stairs again, this time balancing one toe on the skirting board and swinging his weight over the last two steps, just as he used to all those years ago when he helped his big sister.

He rounds the corner past another brand-new handrail and stoops his way up a narrower uncarpeted staircase, catching his head on an exposed rusty steel lintel at the top.

'Bastard!'

He fiddles around and clicks on a naked 100-watt light bulb. He clambers over an inverted peach sink and steps inside one end of a matching bath, squatting down to rummage through the detritus at the other end.

He picks up a bundle of dolls' clothes and brushes the dust off an armless naked doll. 'Ha! "Barbie the..."' He laughs and glances back to the open doorway.

David looks up at the walls; a poster of five boys in tartan and white dangles from one corner above a huddle of teddies. A sheet of hardboard rests in a curve against the wall. He tugs it out and leans it against the bath. It has white roads painted neatly on a green background, and rectangles have been carefully drawn on either side of the roads. He drives his finger along the road. He takes out his phone and thumbs through his contacts till he finds the face of a broad young man in a rugby shirt and the name Danny. He types a short message, adds a couple of emoticons and sends it.

He turns round with a cough and scrambles to the far end of the attic room over a roll of carpet and through another low doorway. He clicks on another bare light.

He leans on a vintage suitcase and crouches in front of two stacks of magazines. He plucks the first from a pile of yellow-spined *National Geographics* and blows the dust off a picture of Santa Claus on the back. He flicks through the second pile, picking out one with a picture of Natalie Wood. It is labelled '*Colour Photography* No. 6 1959. 2s.6d.' Boxes of lenses and camera equipment and a broken tripod lie undisturbed.

He stoops lower under the eaves and pulls out a cardboard box labelled 'David – School'. He takes out the first blue-covered exercise book, stares at the school crest and tries to tear the book in half. He shoves it back in the box and kicks the box further under the eaves.

He crawls to his left and tugs at a white sheet. He stretches and eases out a white wooden box. There is a Little Chef logo hand-drawn on the side. It has two staircases and the inside has been laid out as a café with tabletops made from Formica samples.

Most of the tabletops have come off. He takes one and tries to press it back in place, but it immediately falls off.

He leans further in and pulls out another white object. He drags it all the way out. It is a three-storey car park with ramps between the floors. The walls have stickers – Michelin, Shell and Ford – and 'CAR PARK' has been hand-painted in blue. Black and red streaks stain the walls of the ramps. He caresses them, running his fingers backwards and forwards, reading the stories he used to play with his fingers. He sniffs and shoves his hand in his pocket. He sniffs again and wipes his nose on his sleeve then roughly rubs his eyes.

He stands up, groaning as the blood rushes back to his feet, smacking his head against the naked bulb, which sways from side to side, like a searchlight across solid timber joists and stacks of boxes.

'Ow!'

When the bulb steadies, he stands with his hands on his hips looking round the rest of the attic and brushes a cobweb off his jumper. He bends down and wipes the white painted wood with the sheet. Then he picks up the car park, carries it out of the old part of the attic and clicks the light off.

He glances again at the poster with a smile, ducks out of the attic and heads down the stairs into the daylight humming, with his car park in his arms.

3.0 Family Background and Early Experiences

This section looks at what has made you into the person you are today. In order for us to properly understand where you came from and what family means to you, we need to know about your family of origin, including your birth parents or adopted parents and other significant family members. If you were adopted yourself, you should explain how this has informed your own thoughts about parenting and adoption.

Describe your early memories of your parents. Can you think of key incidents that led to you understanding your relationship with them? How have those relationships evolved over the years?

If there have been any significant bereavements in your family, it is very important that you are completely open about your feelings. Understanding loss is an important part of knowing who we are and will prove invaluable when supporting an adopted child needing to come to terms with their own loss. The death of one's grandparents or parents at any time of life can be a major formative experience and will impact on the way an adopter feels about family.

Complete one for both applicants when assessing a couple.

3.1 Eco Map and Extended Family

It is important for us to have an understanding of the wider support network available to you beyond your immediate family. Please complete your Eco Map (which is covered in the three-day Fostering and Adoption Training and Development Programme) using the template provided. If you don't have access to a computer or have any technical difficulties, your social worker will be able to explain the options available to you.

When we arrange your Support Network Event, we would expect to meet some of the key figures in your Eco Map, especially if they are expected to play a role in childcare.

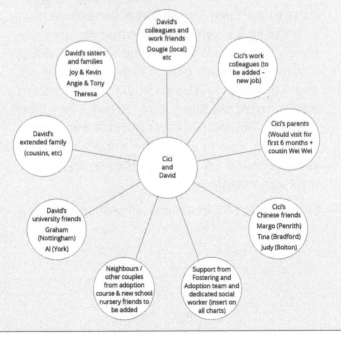

David's Thing

I've got to find my Thing. I must have been about eleven, the only time I ever saw it. Or when I saw the envelope it was in, to be precise: I don't actually know what it was.

It must be in the shed somewhere, New Shed as it's been referred to since Dad built it in 1974. This lock's stubborn. The door needs a good shove.

Stinks of damp wood and sawdust in here. I wonder if it smells like that in his coffin. I don't want to be buried.

He kept that rusty old lawn mower till the end, refused to have an electric one. That's one more thing that can go to the tip now. It's going to take weeks to clear the house out; Mum refused to throw anything away, and by the time she was gone he was too tired. There are Heinz soup labels from the seventies in the kitchen.

Dad was always in his shed in those days. I was the only one allowed; he wouldn't let my sisters in. 'Too dangerous for girls,' he said.

There's a parade of forks, shovels and rakes all standing to attention, and boxes of spanners, pliers and screwdrivers, some as old as me, all useless now without him.

This is where he made doll's houses, jigsaws and Noah's arks. I always expected him to emerge with Chitty Chitty Bang Bang. He made me a bike when I was seven from parts borrowed from the tip, and he painted it red, white and blue. I soared all round the village and along the lanes, imagining I was flying to the moon. It lasted till he bought me a grown-up bike for my twelfth birthday. By then he didn't have time to make things any more. There were too many sisters, and he was always away with work. New Bike still leans against the side of the shed, rusting away. I was so proud the day I wiped all the dirty black oil off it, but he was cross because the oil stopped it rusting. He was planning to refurbish it; another thing left unfinished.

I remember the Thing being on this bench right next to the vice. He used to tease me about torturing me with the vice. They'd have appreciated that at St Peter's. The Thing's not here now. There's a squadron of dead spiders and flies in the cobwebs by the dirty window. When I saw it I asked him what it was and he said, 'Never you mind,' lifted the envelope over my head and hid it on the top shelf.

It isn't on that shelf now. I'm looking for a bulky manila envelope about A4 size, folded in half and thoroughly sealed with Sellotape. He used to get envelopes from the post office in Lymm, and we'd drive the long way round on the motorway. He would get his car tax done there. Once I wanted to look at an Airfix Spitfire but he was in a hurry, and we left with the envelopes without going to the till.

All I could see was that the Thing was an irregular shape and it was heavy from the way he held it. It made a metallic sound when he put it down. It could have been some kind of tool, but what use would that be? I was never handy like Dad.

At the time I thought it might be a gun. Dad was forever telling heroic tales about 'When I was in the army...'

The writing's the only other clue: 'DAVID'S THING' was hand-written on it in thick black marker pen. I think it was Dad's writing, but I can't be sure. He used to draw Diddy Men and treasure maps on cards when I was ill. The 'D' reminded me of the way Mum wrote my name, but I never saw her write in capitals. And she never came in the shed.

Apart from not knowing what it was, it might not have been for me at all. David could have meant me *or* my dad. Not that he was ever referred to by name. He was 'Dad' or 'Daddy' to my sisters, 'Love' to Mum, and occasionally 'Mr Potter', like when he was doing council stuff or that time the police came to the front door. And if the Thing was his, why would he write David on it?

I never understood where he was or what he did when he was working. He went away a lot. He was like James Bond to me. Jack Greenhall's dad actually was an international spy in the sixties, he told me so. But in Cornwall, that summer with the ladybird plague, Dad was discussing strikes in the hotel bar and that didn't sound like something spies would do. We didn't go on holiday the year after. He sold the Rover (Old Car) and didn't buy another car for ages.

At one time I thought it might be a hand like Thing in *The Addams Family*. But the blood would have seeped through the envelope; besides, why would he have a hand in an envelope? By then Dad said I was getting too old for Marvel comics, so it can't have been Thing out of the Fantastic Four, and anyway Thing was made of rock, not metal, and he wasn't my favourite.

When Dad was at home, he always had council meetings in the evenings. I used to listen for the sound of Old Car chugging up the street at night when he came home. They had lots of meetings. He never seemed to be there from about that time, when I was first sentenced to grammar school. Things might have turned out differently if I'd been able to talk to him.

It isn't on any of these shelves. That's the metal sieve he used for getting stones out of the soil. He let me use it to prospect for gold in the sandpit but I only ever found cat poo.

He kept a few spare kitchen tiles, a broken mirror, a corroded radiator and a pair of taps... no, two hot taps. He was forever telling us how lucky we were to have an indoor toilet. 'You don't know you're born,' he always said and, 'We couldn't afford a towel when I was a lad. We had to dry ourselves with a brick.' It was easier when he grew up: National Service then a job for life. He had no idea what went on at school and how complicated life would be after *that* education.

Come to think of it, he was never there for parents' evening. Mum always said work was very busy and what he did was important, but she never looked at me when I asked when he was coming home.

Buried behind all the wood are rows of glass jars full of nails and screws, old tins of paint and varnish, no sign of any envelope. I used to trap wasps in jam jars. If you punched a hole in the metal lid from the outside, they could breathe, but they couldn't get out.

My life was so different to his. I've spent most of my life sitting on the M6. I applied for a job at the council once, but I didn't get an interview. When I asked Steve Clarke, who remembered me from school, he made the usual comments about lots of applicants. Then he said, 'Probably best, given your dad's politics.' I didn't know it was wrong to be Conservative then.

These boxes under the bench are full of off-cuts of wood, parts of toys, odd wheels. It could be buried here but I can't see it… cat pepper, ant powder, weed killer, but no Thing. And there's the chipboard bird table Dad made with me for Scouts.

I used to talk to Mr Beardsley, the Scout leader, about careers. He was on the council too, lived three houses up from us. Then he was run over one night on the way back from a meeting, some drunk driver. His daughters wouldn't come out and play anymore. Angie used to play with them a lot before that. Mum said it was best not to try and talk to them. 'People can be funny when they've had a shock,' she said. Dad was away at the time. He stopped going to council meetings then too. Another thing he was too busy for.

He was going to put that chicken wire round the back of the compost heap, keep animals out; that's where he used the rat poison. He attached some of the same mesh to the garage window to stop people breaking in. I used to throw a tennis ball against the wall like I was Steve McQueen in *The Great Escape*.

I hardly saw Dad those last two years after Mum died. We all visited less after that. It was hard to ring him. He was never much of a talker, and he was quite deaf towards the end.

Eventually, Theresa got it out of him. She was there most often. She lived alone all those years. Prostate cancer. Not that he'd ever talk about it. I didn't know what to do when he was incontinent. I mean, it's awkward, isn't it, when you're in public? That's why I never got round to taking him to the football.

Funny, one of my earliest memories is about a toilet. I sat on the toilet for a wee on the way back from Wales (I wasn't big enough to do stand-up wees) and there was no toilet roll, and Dad said it didn't matter, but I didn't want there to be a dribble, so he wiped it with his hand, and he got really cross and said something about growing up.

I'll probably end up the same way he did. He was always going on about pensions when he was my age. He seemed to stop work very suddenly after that time he'd been so busy. He'd sit in the dining room alone reading at night. Sometimes he'd sit in the dark.

It's cold in here. I need the toilet now, come to think of it. All that dust's getting in my eyes. Anyway, it's impossible to see anything in all this junk. No sign of any envelope.

I should have asked Dad about David's Thing before he died. He might have finally given it to me.

4.0 Childhood and Education

Summarise your educational experiences and how they have influenced your views on the importance of education.

Please give any information you feel may be relevant about your own childhood. What was school like for you? Did you feel accepted? If not, why not? How did you get on with your peers and your teachers? Do you feel that your school experience has influenced how you would raise your own children or an adopted child? What about your teenage years? What did you feel?

Explain how you will make sure that any child is fully supported in their education and how you intend to help them with their development. Do you think education is important for a child? Do you understand the education system? Do you have any professional experience of education? What was your experience of leaving school like? How does that inform how you would manage that experience with an adopted child?

Your relationships with siblings are also important during childhood, so you may wish to reflect on how you were with your brother(s) and sister(s) (if you had any) at that time in your life.

A great deal of information and support is available on the website, including information about nursery and school choices and funding options for adopted children. You will be expected to have researched the local resources such as nurseries and support groups as part of your support network plan.

List the education institutions you have attended in chronological order, along with qualifications gained, on the form below, form 5.2.2 (formerly form EC 101/2). Applicants who have had higher education such as university do not necessarily understand the social and emotional needs of children better, so there is no advantage in having lots of qualifications. We are more concerned with your ability to understand the emotional and social development of a child.

Veritas Nunquam Perit, Part I:
The Last Sister

'Settle down, oiks!' Mr Austin marched into the classroom like he was commanding an army. 'Settle down!'

We always made him ask twice. Tubby Thompson emitted a Silent But Deadly, and Boyle Minor punched his arm. Austin paraded between the rows of desks with his hands behind his back. After a couple of minutes of scraping chairs and general murmuring, the class quietened down.

'The good news, for me, boys, is that today we are going to hear some of *your* inane drivel. And there will be silence.'

This provoked a well-rehearsed communal groan. I pulled my head into my blazer like a tortoise. I had to make sure I was never *embarrassed*. It had taken me months to get over the shame when Kolowski spotted my uninvited erection in biology in the second year.

English was one of the few lessons where you could be exposed. The threat came from one's own work being read out. A great deal of skill was required to avoid that humiliation. The only attempts at creativity were submitted by a clique of arty boys who always wore scarves and CND badges. Their leader, a languid Irish lad called McNair, flaunted long hair and avoided being beaten up because he was so confident in his homosexuality that no one quite knew how to take him.

To avoid exposure I would write only factual material. So, if the topic was 'Write about your home', I'd describe the house and avoid any reference to people, rendering the work worthless. The teacher would skim-read the dreadful essays, scribbling C in red and an occasional *sp* in the margin, until one piece showed a bit of flair and he'd read it out. This meant that McNair and his cronies monopolised the performances, and I could safely shrink into the background. I avoided exposure by writing about nothing interesting and writing it with consistent blandness.

'This week I have a special treat to celebrate the end of term. I have your exam papers!'

Shit shit shit!

I had written something personal. I thought I was safe in the exam.

'That means you all made a special effort. Some of your empty-headed ramblings are almost legible. And I have a pleasant surprise for you. This week's selected essay is not one of our usual... ahem... boys.'

Pause.

'Potty!'

Oh no!

Relieved cheers from everyone else. I hated the way he called me Potty.

'This isn't your usual tiresome descriptive drivel, Potty. You must have been inspired. I never would have thought you had it in you, but then it was inconceivable to me that we'd ever have a *lady* prime minister, God help us.'

Eyebrows raised; jackals ready to devour me. They were all glaring at me. I was burning. I stared at the motto on the cover of my exercise book: *Veritas Nunquam Perit*.

'Potty, you chose the subject of a birth or death in the family. The title of your essay is "The Last Sister".' He looked up for approval. 'Shall we begin?'

I hadn't fully realised yet what a sadist he could be. All I could do was stare at the tear on the back of Simpson's collar and hold my breath.

Austin began in a theatrical tone. '"We had all been looking forward to the baby's birth. It was an important one for me because I hoped that I would finally have a baby brother: I already had enough sisters. I've always felt like an outcast; no wonder in a house full of girls and a school full of prep-school bully boys. They are all such phonies."'

I concentrated on the tiny tunnel I had begun to dig with my compass in a black knot on my desk, while he led a discussion on my obvious reference to Salinger and when a citation was appropriate; not here, apparently. I could hear Austin's voice in the distance but I was tensing my head. A few seconds seemed to go on forever, like holding your breath under water in swimming lessons.

"'...As soon as he came through the front door, the sisters scurried around him like a pair of *naughty kittens*. I was halfway down the stairs when he looked up. I'll never forget the half-smile-half-frown that told me it was another girl a moment before he made the announcement. The sisters squealed and jumped. I turned and slinked back into my bedroom. This was the last baby; I'd never have a brother. I would play my Simon and Garfunkel tape."'

A sarcastic 'Aawww' oozed round the room. I should have quoted The Jam or The Who. The murmuring started even before the obligatory Q&A that always followed a reading. Austin congratulated me for expressing myself so articulately and, to my horror, asked me what the baby was called. They were actually going to publicly disembowel me! Everyone in the world was staring at me. I could smell the salty sweat on my hands as I half covered my face. Silence. I had no choice.

'Er... Imelda Joy, sir.'

Roars of laughter. By the time he called order again I felt physically sick and I had morphed from crimson to olive-green.

'That's a very unusual name, Potty, where did it come from?'

'I... err, that is, my parents let me make a suggestion because... you know, because I wanted it to be a boy and everything, err... so I looked through the Catholic names book that they bought when the previous sister was born.'

'And why, may I ask, did you settle on that name?'

'Err… I think it was an attempt to be unusual, sir. My other sisters have such conservative Christian names… Angela Bernadette… and, erm, Theresa Mary.'

This was also hilarious. Everything was funny to these hyenas. Things could not get any worse. The door opened with a horror movie creak. Brother O'Brien, our class teacher. I could see the veins on my palms.

'No need to rise, boys.' He had a nasal voice.

There was no indication anyone was about to stand up. He floated to the centre of the room. In his habit he moved exactly like a Dalek.

'Ignore me, Mr Austin,' he preached, standing a few inches from Austin's face. 'What are you reading today?'

Austin looked down his long chin at his colleague. 'We have been reading Potter's exam essay about the birth of his sister.'

'Congratulations are in order, Mr Potter! When did this take place?'

I wanted to say, 'During the exam,' and get them on my side, but that would be too brave.

'Err… April the 21st, sir,' I croaked.

'You must share this kind of news with the class in future.'

'Yes, sir.'

A small boy called Sloan made a rasping noise. Brother O'Brien was suddenly upon him. He clubbed Sloan twice with a hard-backed bible, and silence was restored. Sloan sat and stared ahead, trying not to cry. Everyone tried not to look at him.

I wished my pain had been as short-lived. When my ordeal was ended by the deafening bell, I opened the back page of my English book and wrote in capitals:

I WILL NEVER WRITE ANYTHING PERSONAL AGAIN.

5.0 Adult Life: Work History and Finances

Please complete the work history pro forma (Form D2), detailing all employment positions you have ever held, including self-employed and voluntary work. Leave no gaps. For every employer include their full name and address, and the dates you worked there. Highlight any employment where you have worked with children or vulnerable adults. We will need to contact each of these for a reference. We require at least one reference from your current or most recent employer, whatever the nature of the work you undertook with them. You are advised to inform your employer of your plans to adopt. You will be expected to have planned how your work circumstances are relevant to your application to adopt with regards to any anticipated changes after a child is placed with you. There is information in the training folder and on the website about your rights to adoption leave, as well as leave during any bridging period.

The Council does not discriminate on the grounds of a person's income, and we will not undertake any unnecessary investigations into your personal finances. Please complete the Financial Planning pro forma (Form G1) outlining your monthly income and outgoings. You should include all of your regular costs, e.g. rent or mortgage, council tax, utility bills, etc. Please provide originals of your last three months' bank statements and credit card statements, including any loans, overdrafts and savings accounts. Please also provide a copy of your last three months' payslips or HMRC records if you are self-employed. If you have any outstanding County Court Judgments (CCJs) or Individual Voluntary Arrangements (IVAs) or have ever been declared bankrupt or have experienced financial difficulties, please explain fully. Previous circumstances will not automatically preclude you from approval if you can demonstrate that your current circumstances are stable.

You should consider writing a will, if you do not already have one, and revising it when matched. This is especially important for older parents. Your will should show how you have planned for the whole lives of any adopted child. Please also fill in the Nomination form (Form H3) stating whom you have nominated as your next of kin in the event that you should die. This is usually a close family member such as a sibling or parent. Include full name(s), address(es) and contact details, including work telephone numbers. You should seek their consent first as this is a major step to take. They may be required to undergo a DBS check, so we will ask that they complete a consent form for that purpose.

Ten Ten am

'Oh no!'

What's happened? Someone's losing it in the next cubicle. Maybe he's received some bad news. Perhaps he came in here to hide too. Wonder who it was. He's flushed and gone.

I'd better get back too; it's like a prison here. I'm working on an escape plan. You feel like you're constantly on view. People will stare when I cross the room back to my office. You can see it in their eyes: 'We know where you've be-een!' I'll go via the kitchen. Walking back with a mug of coffee hides where I've been.

Stinks in here. Wash my hands, take my time. It's like when you used to come in from the playground at school after it had been snowing outside, and the water was boiling hot, and you could make bubbles with the soap, and your fingers stung. This place is a bit like school, the way the day is marked out in sections. I usually come to the gents at about ten. Then get a bite to eat at about twelve-thirty. When I have a quiet moment at four, I usually feel better. The last two hours of the day are easier.

The door's opening. If I don't turn round, I might not have to speak.

'Mornin'.'

'Morning.'

One of the accountants. Better get out of here.

Kitchen smells like someone's been cooking sprouts. Are there any clean mugs? Dark-haired Slim Girl grins as she opens a cupboard. Was that a bit of a flirt? Be realistic; I'm old enough to be her dad. There is one girl, Louise. Her skirts are always really tight. It can be hard not to be distracted, what with Cici's medical problems.

Is the water in this boiler hot enough? Low-fat milk, yuck. Make it extra strong; it's going to be a long day. I must do something else... write, maybe. Most days there are meetings, and all I have to do is sit there and look intelligent. During one meeting I wrote a three-page story.

Look at all these people in rows staring at screens, huddling, muttering; IT nerds, customer service teams, supervisors. Do they all feel the same way? Are they also pretending and hoping no one notices? Did they have dreams about making a difference? Do they do it for their kids?

The HR Manager (Business Partner for Employee Engagement) slinks past. Expensive trouser-suit.

'I'd like to touch base this morning,' she whispers.

'Of course, Denise, we have the meeting at half past.'

'Perhaps we could diarise a meeting?'

'Fine.' If I haven't quit by then.

Most of the time she just *tells* me what she is doing. They are all like that, the senior managers. They pretend they're including me. I'll nip into Dougie's office. He's the only one that sees the absurdity of it all. 'Facilities and Logistics' is his bag. He admits he isn't sure what that covers.

'Morning, Dougie.'

'Have you got all your ducks in a row ready for the Friday Fright?'

'Should be safe today. Heather cocked up with the bank.'

'Good, keeps you and me out of it.'

'An odd thing just happened in the gents...'

'How is the, erm...?'

'Painful, thanks. Anyway, there I am hiding in trap two, and a voice yells out from trap one: "Oh noooo!"'

'Sure it wasn't you?'

'Might have been.'

'Any further thoughts on your escape plan?'

'I'm working my way up to it. Cici's been great. She's had her promotion, and there's enough put away for a year. I can always get a job if we have another go at IVF.'

'Is she all right now?'

'You know Cici, she's strong. We might try again next year.'

'Fancy a game of Boardroom Bingo?'

'It'll be a quick one today. James has been shouting "Vertical Integration" round the office all week.'

'He's got the jargon, I'll give him that. By the way, I'm trying to embed the word "embed" into the vernacular, so try and use it if you get a chance. I've already dropped it to Sir a couple of times.'

'I will, good word… *embed*. I'm going to hide till the meeting.'

Shut them all out. I could do with staying on my feet. I can't stand here gazing out of the window all day. Or maybe I could. It's not as if it makes any difference. Is that blurry face in the window me?

Better have a look at these emails. I wish they would put a subject that tells you what it's really about and spare me the 'URGENT'. It's like they don't think I'm smart enough to determine by myself which things are a matter of life and death (none of these, actually). In the end, everything has several red exclamation marks.

Not going to Health and Safety conference. Delete. Request for approval of office equipment; what box do I tick? It's a bloody chair. If someone says they want a special orthopaedic support, let them have it.

Paul Newman's grinning at me from the wall. Cici cut the picture out of a movie magazine for me. She understands. What would Cool Hand Luke have done if he was here? What did Dad feel like when he retired? At the end, did he look back and think it was all pointless? Certainly didn't help his health.

Here they come. You'd think people would interpret a closed door as an indication you want to be left alone, but they just knock once while they're opening it and start talking.

'Good morrow, young sir!'

It's Graham; he does marketing (Strategic Client Development), tremendous moustache. His voice goes up and down so much he almost sings.

'Am I interrupting you?'

'Morning, Graham. I am rather busy…'

'I won't take more than the merest smidgen of your time.'

Smidgen? 'What's on your mind, Graham?'

'Ticking off my actions from last week, wanted to leave you the draft strategy review for you to per*use* at your leisure.'

I can hardly lift it. 'Am I required to respond to this?'

'I'd be *very* grateful for any input you *deign* to proffer.'

'Do you have a deadline for this?'

'The draft needs to be signed off by month end. I'd be delighted if we could have a little session next week and dance through it together, as it were.'

'If I get chance, I'll have a look…'

'Tickety boo! *Tempus fugit* and all that…'

He leaves my office and passes the door handle to the next one like a relay baton. It's Ms. HR again, Denise (she insists on it being pronounced 'Deneeez').

'How are you, David?' she asks.

'Busy as always, I really need to…' I've still got the strategy document in my hand. I wave it to show how heavy it is. Might be useful after all.

'I'd like to diarise something about the employee survey.'

'Is it that time of year again?'

And… she's off. Straight into last year's return rate and how important it is *strategically*. I'll kiss the first person that comes in here and doesn't use the word 'strategy'. She wants to solution the churn.

Louise is loitering by the door, bearing paper. Deneeez looks down at her and promises me an Outlook invitation.

'Louise. How can I help you?' Smile.

'Keith asked me to bring you the flash figures.'

Column after column of meaningless numbers. She's waiting for me to speak. 'Thanks, Louise. I'll take a look at them later.' Charming as ever.

She wiggles out. Tight skirt. I wonder...

Now it's the Commercial Director, James. He is smarter than most of them, but strides around the office yelling into his mobile: 'Blah blah blah blah, strategy blah blah blah...'

'James, can we do this another time? I need to look at these figures...'

'Blah blah, blah, on the radar. Shall I shut the door?'

'Thank you.'

What are these numbers? Ah, we've made a million pounds this quarter. That's me on for a bonus then. I can buy a gun and blow my brains out.

I need to stand up again.

What time is it? The fingers on that clock seem to be stuck. They are making a wide 'V' at me. Ten past ten and I've already been here over two hours. Maybe I should hang myself with the company tie from the corporate flagpole outside my window. Health and Safety would have to do a Risk Assessment. At least I've got Cici. But what good am I to her when I'm disappointed every day?

It's spitting. I haven't seen Danny for a fortnight. His mum changed the weekends. He looks so happy in that photo from when we went to Wales. That's what's missing. If we had a kid, I could probably survive it. How could I be a parent feeling like this? I need to do something else. Which drawer did I put that *How to Write a Novel* book in?

Graham's back. 'Meeting's now in meeting room two. Thought I'd flag it up, keep you in the loop.'

'Thanks, Graham.' I want to add, 'I'll only come if you shave off your moustache.'

Can I have a moment to think? Nope, here's that grouchy office manager, Mrs Jennings. Always frowns. I can't work out if it's an affectation to make herself look managerial, or if she really is angry. She's got a delivery: boxes of business cards with the new corporate logo. Let's see what I look like in print. Nice cards, embossed.

DJ POTTER MBA CIM MIHT
DIRECTOR OF IMPROVEMENT, CHANGE & KNOWLEDGE SHARING

No one, me included, has any idea what that means.
Ten twenty.

* * *

So, that was my last meeting. The Friday Fright is Sir's opportunity to vent. He uses it as a vehicle for reducing and humiliating. I used to be someone here. I had ideas. Now I just kill the days.

It was the turn of Heather, the Finance Director, who hadn't *actioned* the extension of the bank facility, causing a bit of embarrassment for Sir when he met the CEO of one of our main suppliers at a golf do. He was on quite good form, doesn't raise his voice with Heather as much as the others. She's smart enough not to answer back. He's a Yorkshireman, tends to talk very loudly.

'I would prefer to avoid being left with my dick out on the golf course because we can't pay people since one of my Directors has – what word did you use? – *overlooked* it.'

She sat there going red. Dougie slipped me a folded piece of paper with the word 'EMBED' on it. Sir continued.

'I am reminded of the chairman's favourite phrase. If you can't change the people, change the people.'

James explained something about the new structure including the words 'vertical integration', which caused Dougie to cough noisily. Then Sir banged on a bit about 'incentivisation', and that he had something about performance that he wanted to 'embed' in the culture. I was in trouble after that. Dougie kept chinking his pencil against his glass to get my attention, but I wouldn't look up. Then it happened. James was droning on about 'low-hanging fruit' and then he said the word 'dovetail'.

'House!' I yelled and started to laugh. Belly-ache, can't-get-your-breath laughing.

Sir gawked at me. The others were all a bit confused, apart from Dougie. From what I could see between the tears, he was struggling not to laugh and, I'd like to think, a bit proud. No one joined in, so eventually I stopped. Sir was stood up with his hands on his hips.

'Have you quite finished?'

'Yes, thank you for asking. I think I'll go home now. I can't carry on, it's too silly.'

'Have you gone completely out of your mind?'

'Quite the opposite, Arthur.'

'What?'

'What we've got here is failure to communicate.' I did the voice of the warden in *Cool Hand Luke* as closely as I could – a sort of high-pitched southern drawl.

'If you walk out of my meeting, that's the end of your career here!'

'Good, you've worked that out, have you? Well done. Before I go, may I say that I've never especially enjoyed the yelling? And the motivational technique of threatening physical violence is a tad out of date.'

He looked like he was going to burst, but everyone was sitting in silence, looking down, so I carried on.

'While I'm at it... James, congratulations on being voted Cock of the Year – they ran a poll. Denise, "solution" is not a verb. And Graham? Tickety boo!'

* * *

So, here I am with my cardboard box. The rain's stopped. The photo of Danny and the Newton's Cradle Mum bought me are about the only things I need to keep. Take the books out of the drawer. James Joyce, I'll have time to tackle him now. I don't need the tie, that can go in the bin. Here's Dougie.

'What the fook? I thought he was going to strike you.'

'After he said "embed", I was struggling.'

'I'm proud of you, mate, you finally did it.'

'Was I bit harsh on the others?'

'I think you held back quite well. Bit disappointed you missed me out. What are you going to do now?'

'They've got to pay me three months, and Cici's doing well these days.'

'You could probably retrieve it if you wanted to. I could soften him up.'

'Thanks, Dougie, but I don't want to end up like Jimmy.'

'God rest him.'

'Do you want my company tie?'

'For me? I tell you what, I'll have your *Cool Hand Luke* picture, if you don't need it. "What we've got here is failure to communicate!"' He exaggerates the voice more than me.

'Uncanny. It'll be good to spend more time with Danny. If me and Cici ever do have a child, I don't want the hours and the grief of working here, and I've waited too long to do the writing thing.'

'What are you thinking?'

'I've got that offer at to do the MA at Lancaster. I can write blogs for companies to earn a few quid. Maybe I'll teach and write, finish that novel.'

'I didn't know you were writing a novel.'

'All right, start a novel.'

'I'd better get back.'

'You're going to stay then?'

'I'm in it for life, mate, too many years in the pension and the bairns to think about. Thanks for the picture. I'll see you in the pub.'

'Tickety boo.'

6.0 Adult Life: Relationship History

It is important for us to understand your previous relationships, so that we can properly assess the kind of person you are. Please complete the Relationship Chronology pro forma in 6.2 (formerly form F2) and list all of your previous relationships, including every relationship you have had since the age of 16, whether or not you were married or cohabited. Include the last known address of each partner in the space provided and the dates of the start and end of the relationship.

The Council is committed to providing support for all applicants, regardless of their gender or sexual orientation. We actively encourage applications for adoption from all parts of the community and have been very successful supporting members of the LGBT+ community in this respect.

If you have been married or been in a civil partnership or cohabited before, it will be necessary to contact all previous partner(s) for a reference, regardless of the timescale or circumstances. However, please be assured we understand and accept that people are exes for a reason! We will comply with the Council's policy of confidentiality, but your social worker will want to discuss with you all aspects of previous relationships, so that they can develop an informed opinion about your whole personality. In some circumstances your social worker may feel it necessary to speak to your former partner(s) or meet them face to face, as well as seeking a written reference. As a minimum, written references will be sought from everyone you have cohabited with or been married to.

If you are a single applicant, you must consider how a future relationship might impact on any adopted child and/or explain your decision to be a single parent. You will need to discuss the implications of any potential relationship in the future and the steps that will need to be taken to safeguard any adopted child(ren).

John Peel Day

'Happy John Peel Day.'

'Happy what, Dougie?'

'October the thirteenth, it's John Peel day. Ten years today since the first one.'

'The stuff you know, Dougie.'

'Here ye go.' He hands David a pint of Theakstons.

There are seven people in the Gaunt, including the barmaid: normal for 7pm on a Tuesday.

'A toast then,' David says. 'To the man that brought us The Ramones.'

'And The Undertones.' Dougie raises his glass. 'Teenage kicks!'

'Teenage kicks.'

'He has a line from that on his grave, you kna.'

'Really? I love that he played it twice. You know the story about Billy Bragg…?'

'Course. Peel says he's hungry on air; Billy Bragg turns up with a mushroom biryani and his record. The rest is history.'

'What about Peel playing the mandolin on *Maggie May*?'

'Aye, that's true.'

'Anyway, I've got a story about the thirteenth of October…'

'Let me get sat down first.' Dougie settles himself on a worn corner seat beneath a series of framed beer mats on mustard-coloured walls. A row of brass instruments is gathering dust on a shelf.

David says, 'It's about coincidence. Three stories happen simultaneously.'

'Like one of them Robert Altman fillums?'

'And it's true.'

'Alreet, I like a true story,' Dougie says.

'Let me tell you all of it before you say anything.'

'Long as you get to the end before I finish me pint.'

'And promise you'll keep an open mind.'

'Alreet.'

'So, it's Friday the thirteenth of October, 1995, eleven fifty pm. It's raining. There's a taxi at a roundabout. Inside the taxi is a smart black raincoat. Inside the raincoat is a young woman. She's near a business park on the A560 in Altrincham. Her new flat is an old couple's converted garage in Hale…'

'Nice details, canny lad…'

'There are tears in her eyes. She's been out in Manchester with her friends, but she's had a phone call and had to rush home. The married man she's having an affair with – her boss – has just been kicked out by his wife. It's his fortieth birthday. His wife's waited till their friends are about to leave his party and announced he's been having an affair and he's moving out. She's reached into the under-stairs cupboard where she's hidden two suitcases full of his clothes and chucked them out onto their well-manicured lawn.'

'Serves 'im right.'

'They argue, but she threatens he'll never see his teenage daughter again if he doesn't go quietly. The daughter has some mental health issues.'

'Harsh.'

'So, the woman in the taxi's had to go home. She's not happy. She's only left her own husband the previous weekend. They've hardly been married five years. She's feeling guilty, her parents are angry with her, she's about to lose her job…'

'On account of her sleeping with the boss, like?'

'In those days a woman would have no chance. She isn't even sure if she wants to be with this man. She wants kids, and he's had the snip...'

'Ouch.'

'All she knows is that from this moment, Friday the thirteenth of October, 1995, eleven fifty pm, her life will never be the same again. There's the life she had before and the new life that's yet to begin. This is the pivotal moment in her life.'

'Go on.'

'She hears a siren, the flashing blue lights of an ambulance approach the roundabout...'

'Drama!'

'Inside the ambulance is a faux fur coat. Inside the coat is another young woman.'

'Let me guess, it's a turning point in her life too? It being a roundabout an' all.'

'Let me tell it! She's on her way to the hospital, she's gone into labour. Twins, she's having. She doesn't know this yet, but they'll make a mess of things at the hospital.'

'No surprise there... Sorry.'

'They're going to cut her open without a general anaesthetic. The twins will both die, one of each. She'll nearly bleed to death.'

'She loses both bairns? Breaks your heart.'

'Things are going to go wrong for her. It'll take her years to recover. The father will slap her around, she'll end up on her own with another baby a couple of years later, a boy. And she will drink.'

'Nowt wrong with that.'

'I mean bad drinking. Remember Fat Dave?'

'Aye, God rest his soul.'

'That bad. I mean neat-vodka, bottles-hidden-in-the-toy-cupboard, arrests-for-drunk-and-disorderly, banned-from-driving, smash-a-guy's-glasses-off-his-face kinda drinking.'

'Sounds like another story you told me. What about the little fella?'

'He grows up big and strong, ends up at university.'

'As long as no more bairns come to any harm.'

'Anyway, she doesn't know any of this yet. All she knows is that from this moment, Friday the thirteenth of October, 1995, eleven fifty pm, her life will never be the same again. There's the life she had before and the new life that's yet to begin.'

'I can see what you're doing…'

'She can't see out, but she hears the hiss of the brakes of a coach.'

'She'd notice that while she's in labour, from inside an ambulance, like?'

'Anyway, at the roundabout is a coach. Inside the coach is a white woollen coat with a hood and a Hello Kitty logo on the front. Inside the hoodie is another young woman. She's Chinese… Don't make that face, Dougie.'

'Sorry. I think I know where you're going.'

'Anyway, she's a student, just got off the plane. She's heading north to university.'

'Here in Lancaster?' Dougie asks.

'Carlisle.'

'St Martins College?' Dougie frowns. 'Like in *Common People*?'

'University of Northumbria,' David says. 'I think it was a different St Martin's in the song. You'd know this, Dougie: is it true Jarvis is related to *Joe* Cocker?'

'Nah, common misconception cause they're both from Sheffield.'

'So's Richard Hawley.'

'And Paul Carrack,' Dougie adds.

'Did you know he was in Squeeze?'

'Did he do the vocals on *Up the Junction*?'

'Very good. Meanwhile, back at the junction in question…'

'Why's she at this roundabout again?'

'It's on the way to the M6 from the airport – least it was in ninety-five when they were widening the M56. I was working for that contractor in Salford then. You'd go that way to Wythenshawe hospital from Sale on the A5144. Or from Manchester to Hale, it's quicker than going through Altrincham.'

'All of which is riveting, Mr Tarmac. What about the lass on the bus?'

'It's her first time away from home. Afterwards she'll remember the cat's eyes on the motorway, her first memory of the UK. She doesn't know this yet, but she'll never go back to China. She'll be lonely and meet the wrong type of man. She'll have a dog's life, washing dishes in a restaurant till four in the morning while she studies. She'll have health issues too, gynaecological.'

'Too much information...'

'Anyway, she doesn't know any of this yet. All she knows is that from this moment, Friday the thirteenth of October, 1995, eleven fifty pm, her life will never be the same again. There's the life she had before and the new life that's yet to begin.'

'Same as the other two?'

'Exactly. She hears the siren and looks out into the rain. She sees a typical English black taxi and an ambulance, a detail she'll recall years later.'

'So what's the point?'

'So, three vehicles are waiting at a roundabout, inside the three vehicles are three coats, inside the three coats are three women, each at the pivotal moment of their lives, Friday the thirteenth of October...'

'...1995, eleven fifty pm.'

'You've got it.'

'So are they going to become friends?'

'No, they never meet. But their fates are intertwined forever.'

'So what's the connection?'

'Haven't you guessed it?'

'Something to do with bairns?'

'Could be – they all have problems having children, but that's not it.'

'Put us out of me misery.'

'I need a drink first.'

'Allow me to visit Oliver while you get 'em in.'[1]

David heads to the bar. Dougie farts loudly in unison with the groan of the door of the gent's toilet. A live band is playing Eighties songs. David sings along to *Heaven Knows I'm Miserable Now* as he delivers two pints.

'I haven't heard Morrissey for yonks,' says Dougie. 'Did you see that fillum about Factory Records the other night?'

'Wasn't there an argument about Ian Curtis?'

'A lot of it was fabricated. Did you ever get to the Hacienda? You lived near Manchester, didn't you?'

'Altrincham. No, I never did. I've met more people that say they saw The Smiths than people that saw The Smiths.'

'I never saw 'em, either. I saw Billy Bragg at Glastonbury – that was '95.' Dougie swigs his beer and leans forward. 'So, these three women, I reckon you must've known 'em all.'

'Yep.' David gazes deep into his beer and breathes in. 'I married all three of them.'

'Howay, man!' Dougie looks around the room. 'Let me get this straight. You're gonna try and convince me that the posh bird from down south, *and* Danny's mam, *and* the present lovely missus were all at the same place at the same time on a particular mystical night?'

---

[1] Above the urinals in Lancaster's Ye Olde John o'Gaunt pub, there is a soft pad made from an old leather seat cover, designed for the customer to rest his head on while urinating. An accompanying small plaque bears the words, 'Rest in Peace, In Memory of the Late Oliver Reed.'

'Yep, twenty years ago today. Friday the thirteenth of October, 1995.'

'Get away!'

'Listen, Danny's mum always got worse at that time of year. Thirteenth of October, that was the date. I went with her to the grave in Walton: small headstone with their names in gold, two tiny flowerpots. There was a rose beside it, the last pink flowers just hanging on. Alice was a mess even years later.'

'Nobody deserves that.'

'She must have gone that way to the hospital from where she lived then. She told me she saw a clock as she was wheeled into the ward at exactly midnight. Alice knew something was wrong – thought it was fate or something. She relived that night over and over.'

'Poor lass. You ever hear from her?

'Once in a while – you know, with Danny. Sober now, met a nice bloke.'

'Whole new experience then. What about the first one?'

'Pippa. Says it on the decree nisi: she admitted adultery, said they'd cohabited since that date. I had to find the divorce papers 'cause that social worker from the adoption department wouldn't believe me.'

'Any news about that?

'None. You know what local authority admin's like. So the boss man was co-respondent on the form and his date of birth was the thirteenth of October.'

'So she was the *first* wife?'

'Yes. Wendy phoned me that night when everyone had left the party. Couldn't wait to tell someone…'

'Hang on, lad, have I missed an episode? Who's Wendy again?'

'Wendy was the boss's wife. You'll have forgotten, but you suggested I call her.'

'Well, there's so many women…'

'Anyway, we knew each other.'

'Knew? In the biblical sense, like?'

'We were friendly, went to see Paul Carrack together in Manchester.'

'You've had some tales, you.'

'I knew it was ten to twelve 'cause I'd just got in when Wendy rang and it took twenty minutes to walk home from the Vine. They kept playing the Happy Mondays 'cause they'd just split up. I remember it was raining.'

'And the last one, the present post-holder?'

'I've seen the travel documents. She was due the week before, but there was a mix-up with the visa. She kept the tickets because it was one of the most important days of her life.'

'I see, and you just happened across this paperwork lying around?'

'She showed it me. When we were filling in those adoption forms, Cici had to find her old addresses. That's when I realised the connection.'

'I'll have to do a bit of work on the chronologies. What was the first one called again?'

'Pippa. We split up in ninety-five. Went to France, said goodbye to her family, shared out the furniture.'

'So how old was she?'

'Twenty-eight then. Shame, her family were lovely.'

'And Danny's away to university now so he's eighteen. That means…?'

'He was one when I met his mum in ninety-eight.'

'So she would have been…?'

'Alice was twenty-eight.'

'I see. And the present incumbent, Cici, would have been student age?'

'She's coming up to forty now…'

'So she was also about twenty-eight when she met you?'

'Listen, she told me the first thing she saw was a black cab and an ambulance. She even took a photo out of the window of the coach.'

'Did they have smartphones then?'

'No, but the camera had been invented.'

'In China, probably. Why would she want a photo of that?'

'First thing she ever saw in England.'

'I thought the cat's eyes were her first memory?'

'She hadn't got as far as the motorway yet; she was only five minutes out of the airport. The flight landed at five past eleven according to the ticket. Allow for baggage reclaim, customs, find the coach, set off about quarter to.'

'Still, it's all a bit implausible.'

'I've got documents that prove it! And in each case that was the moment that defined their life!'

'You're doing Jeff Goldblum hands again...'

'It's true!'

'But the suggestion that they were all at one roundabout at exactly ten to twelve on the same night is a bit far-fetched.'

'I'm just reporting it as it happened.'

'And in each case they chose to marry you, which is in and of itself remarkable.'

'Thank you very much.'

'I'll look it up... October, thirteenth, 1995, day of week... your round.'

'Nice try, it's you.'

'I'm busy looking this up!'

'Then will you believe me?'

'It's not me you've gotta convince, mate. I kna' your history, apart from the graphic details of the mysterious episode that you've somehow omitted to tell me.'

'Have you found it?'

'What do you kna'! October thirteenth, ninety-five... *was* a Friday.'

'See.'

'Says author Henry Roth died that day *and*... the first ever photograph of a comet was thirteenth of October, 1892. Guess what was number one.'

'Pulp? Oasis?'

'Def Leppard, *When Love and Hate Collide*.'

'Appropriate.'

'And... Here's one. Pamela Anderson was rushed to hospital with flu-like symptoms on the thirteenth of October, 1995... says here *twenty-eight-year-old* Baywatch babe...'

'See! All these women...'

'Aye, except you never actually married Pamela Anderson.'

'She had a cold.'

'Lucky escape. It'll be all that running around in bikinis. Look at this. Henry Roth's short stories were published by St Martins...'

'It's all connected!'

'All them things happened on John Peel Day twenty years ago. That, or you're making it up as you go along. How's that beer coming along? It's gonna be a long night.'

'Here. Cast your CSI eyes over this photo while I'm gone...'

7.0 Experience of Loss and Separation

Adoptive children may be vulnerable and have issues with attachment, so you need to be able to show how you have managed situations in the past where you may have suffered from loss or separation yourself.

If you have had previous relationships that have ended for whatever reason, it is important that you reflect now on what happened and are able to show how you have learned from your mistakes and developed strategies for avoiding making the same mistakes again. A previous divorce or separation will not necessarily reduce your chances of being approved but you will need to demonstrate that you have understood what went wrong and how you would avoid the same situation arising in the future.

It is critical that you have a good understanding of attachment issues and how a child's experience of relationships can impact on future relationships. It may mean they find it hard to accept care from an adoptive parent or other adults. How would that make you feel?

Loss and separation occur in many forms. You may have felt sadness about losing members of your own family or moving to new places. As you will know from the Fostering and Adoption

Training and Development Programme, this is a vital part of understanding yourself and becoming equipped to manage adoption and/or fostering.

Explain your own experiences of loss and separation and how that informs your skills as a prospective adopter.

Green Gables

It had only taken us a couple of hours round the M25 and up the M11 to get back to Green Gables. The village was the same as always, with pink pansies in hanging baskets dangling from leaning Tudor houses; funny how the baskets up north never seem to thrive like that. The incline of ancient walls washed with pastel shades of terracotta and blue seemed to be perfectly designed to nestle between the handsome oaks and mature sycamores that line the narrow streets.

I'd always loved the crunching sound as I pulled onto the gravel drive, and I'd learnt the knack of lifting the wrought iron gates simultaneously so the bolts slotted into their holes.

Pippa was quickly out of the car, leaving me to sort everything out as usual. She hugged her mum while I unloaded our matching suitcases, which meant lifting out the camping gear. I scratched her case, the larger one, on the exhaust, leaving a long black scar.

Her father, Henry, came to help and offered a formal handshake while we exchanged awkward greetings. 'Good trip?' he asked, prompting me to describe the traffic all the way from Calais. Pippa and her mum disappeared into the kitchen, nattering away. Would she tell her?

Thankfully, Digger was home from Iraq and it was too early for him to have started drinking. 'The prodigal brother-in-law returns,' he grinned, pulling me into a bear hug. His father gave a disapproving look at his youngest child's affected cockney slur.

'You buying me a pint after dinner then?' I asked.

'I should coco, bruv!'

At least there was that to look forward to. Digger could be a bit of an idiot, but his permanent smirk was exactly what I needed, and I'd told him what was going on before we went. We'd probably be having fish for dinner, it being a Friday, and summer pudding because her mum had got it into her head that it was my favourite. She hugged me as I went into the warm kitchen. The Aga was on, as always. I had to loosen my collar.

'You've certainly caught the sun!' she said. Pippa didn't join in; she hadn't mentioned my tan once. Her mind must have been somewhere else. She was busying herself with the dog.

'Yes, the weather was fantastic,' I said. 'What's it been like here?'

'We had a spot of rain on Tuesday, but otherwise we've had a bit of an Indian summer. I've made your favourite, summer pudding.'

I looked for a knowing smile from Pippa. She didn't look up from the dog until Norbert scuttled across the tiles to greet me himself, wetting my hand and my leg.

'You must tell us *all* about it,' her mum said.

I wandered back to the car to get the AA road atlas of France, on which I had marked our route. I could kill the half hour before dinner, eat, then escape to the pub. The atlas was in the pocket behind the passenger seat. I felt my diary as I stretched round to reach it. I held it for a moment, then shoved it deep into the pocket.

Henry peered at the map over his glasses as I described our trip through Normandy and down the west coast of France. 'Oh, yes, I remember Honfleur, pretty little harbour,' he said. 'What year was that, Bunny?'

I'd never quite dared to call my mother-in-law Bunny. Her blue eyes widened and she smiled. 'It was when the boys were still pre-school; Pippa must have been about five.'

So, it's not only me that'll remember Honfleur for the rest of my life. I've images etched in my mind of a merry-go-round, the fishing boats, the *plats de fruits de mer* we shared (best seafood I'd ever had), the delicate white wine, Gaillac, and the full moon and a thousand stars. And I remember Pippa refusing to kiss me. 'Let's not spoil this,' she had said when I moved towards her.

'David, help Henry set the table, will you?' Bunny said. 'You're in your usual place. Pippa, go and see if you can find that brother of yours.'

'Where's the other one?' I asked.

'Jeremy? He's off at some *rave* tonight; cramming it all in before he sets off for Antarctica.'

I can't imagine what that isolation must feel like, though I'd had some lonely moments in the car these last two weeks.

Henry had already laid out the silver cutlery. I hadn't paid much attention when he told me the history of the dining table every Christmas. It was one of those antiques, Louis Quatorze or Quinze. I did know that a red wine stain would be like crashing a car or killing the dog.

'Why don't you be in charge of the wine?' Henry said, nodding at a bottle of Chardonnay. He was always friendly to me but he couldn't help but sound like a senior officer when he asked you to do something.

'We've brought back a case of Saint-Émilion, last year's.'

'Marvellous, one can't beat a good claret.'

Soon we were chomping our way through Bunny's fish pie, Digger and me taking turns to top up each other's wine glasses. She can drive tomorrow, I thought. It's her turn, and I'm not going to get through this night sober.

I was forced to eat a huge portion of summer pudding, which was too tangy and fought with the wine. I picked at the cheese while Pippa recounted how the farmer/restaurateur at Quimper drew the menu on the tablecloth and how, when I'd pointed at the cow he'd drawn she'd rattled off a few sentences in French and he came back with a Chateaubriand that had not been cooked at all. '*Bleu*' they call it; my word's 'raw'. She told them about the campsites and the night I cut my finger and we both had uncontrollable fits of laughter at the enormous bandage she applied. But she didn't mention the diary.

I'd decided to write a diary for the first time in my twenty-nine years. It was also the first time I'd written anything personal since school. I'd crammed my thoughts between the lines of last year's McAlpine Construction pocket diary with an IKEA pencil. I'd written everything from the music on the radio to my conflicting emotions as we drove through the endless French countryside. We counted Norbert Dentressangle trucks all the way to Bordeaux. (Fifty-three… no, really).

On the last night we sat by the riverbank behind our tent with a plastic jug of Médoc, and she persuaded me to let her read the diary. By the second glass I caved. She could still get her way. I quoted a line from a Del Amitri song about selling my soul to sit and watch her smoke. She sighed and opened the diary. She didn't look up once and only made a couple of disapproving grunts. I sat and chain-smoked. When she'd finished about an hour later, she closed it, handed it back and lit up.

'So, what do you think?'

'It's very well written.'

We didn't make eye contact during dinner except once when I caught her glance as I poured a large glass of port and topped up Digger's, breaching the anti-clockwise rule. She rolled her eyes at me, so I turned to the antique dresser and the two orange-brown Kutani vases I'd always liked. I had the oddest thought; they'd have ended up with us eventually when the oldies (as she called them) died. That wasn't going to happen now.

Half a bottle of wine and the port guided me safely through dinner. Digger was tugging my sleeve before the formalities of clearing up started. I half-heartedly offered to do the washing up. Henry began to say what a good egg that would make me until

Bunny explained things to him with her eyes, and Digger and I were off into the village.

I took a cigarette off him before we reached the gate.

'If you ask me, I think she's being a silly bitch,' he said. 'Have you decided what's gonna 'appen?'

'Dunno, our kid. She says she needs a bit of time to decide, but I think it's too late. Look, can we talk about something else? I just fancy getting pissed and having a game of cards. I'll deal with all that when we get home.'

'You know you can always call me, don't you, mate?'

'I know, but I think the way it works is you keep your own books and relatives. She'll probably bring *him* next year.'

'Fack off!'

He pushed the pub door open and the familiar murmur blanketed me. Before I reached the bar he'd already shaken hands with several of his friends. We'd be here until closing time then cards back at the house. I could gamble away my last holiday cash.

By the time I'd blown £20 at three-card brag my head was hurting, and the top half of the lounge was full of dense smoke. I made my excuses. Digger beamed while he dealt.

'Remember what I said.' Then he did that phone thing with his left hand. I nodded, but we both knew.

I sneaked into Pippa's room and crawled in silently beside her. I thought of the first time we sneaked around at night here… one of the buttons came off her blouse and we bumped heads looking for it and both got the giggles.

I lay on my back at the outer edge of the bed. She rolled over to the far side without speaking. I was exhausted after the journey and three pints of Adnams on top of the wine and port were enough to send me into a deep sleep for the first time in two weeks.

* * *

When I woke, the sun was yelling through the window and my mouth tasted of tar and cheese. Pippa was nowhere in sight. I had to hurry to the bathroom.

I said good morning to her parents as I poured myself a mug of strong coffee. Digger was always louder and later than me, so I never felt the need to apologise for an occasional big drink. Besides, it didn't really matter anymore.

I held my coffee in both hands as I stepped out into the garden. My normal pattern was to stroll the hundred yards to the great old oak tree at the bottom where the horses would come and greet me, then I'd stride back up to the house. Today I sat on Uncle Oliver's bench facing the kitchen with the sun on my back. The bench matched the one he'd made for our wedding present. Would she take that too?

Norbert scampered up to me with his rubber ring. They seem to be especially stupid hounds, Bassets, but at least if you ignored him the first time he understood that you didn't want to play. I didn't used to like dogs.

'All right, daft dog. One throw.'

Bunny shuffled out of the kitchen, a bit hesitant. She had such a lovely smile; I doubt Pippa will look that good at fifty-seven. Why couldn't my mum be more like her?

'It's going to be a lovely day. Shame you have to go so soon.'

'Better get off early, beat Birmingham before lunchtime.'

She sat next to me. Norbert followed her. We had one of those pregnant pauses. I didn't know what to say, so I waited for her to break first.

'You know you'll always be welcome here, don't you?'

Somehow that went straight to the back of my eyes, and I had to clear my throat before I could reply. She'd talked to Pippa. I put my hand on hers; her skin was so soft, like Grandma's when I was small.

'I will miss you all, even daft dog...'

'Oh, you don't need to feel...' She saw my head shake.

'This will be the last time I ever come here.' I looked away out of embarrassment, and when I turned back two tears were having a race down her cheeks.

Pippa appeared and the moment was gone. I stood, took a last look at the garden and headed straight through the house to where our bags were standing to attention by the front door. I lifted one case in each hand and left the house.

By the time I had reorganised the car boot everyone had come out, apart from Digger who was still sleeping off his drink. Henry firmly shook my hand. I got in the car. Pippa squeezed her mum. Henry grabbed Norbert so he didn't run in front of the car when Pippa reversed out too fast. I wound down the window as the gate clanged shut.

'Say bye to the boys for me, won't you.'

They looked at each other. Bunny smiled and waved. Then Pippa drove us away.

8.0 Understanding of Addiction, Violence and Abuse

As you will have learned from your three-day Fostering and Adoption Training and Development Programme, many potential adopted children will have had some experience of neglect or deliberate abuse, often as a consequence of alcohol misuse or drug addiction.

What have you learned about these issues, and what coping strategies do you have? How do you plan to effectively manage the development of a child who may have birth issues such as foetal alcohol syndrome or developmental issues as a result of maternal drug addiction, for example?

If you have experienced any difficulties yourself in the past with addiction, please describe your history – honesty is always best. This will not necessarily prohibit your application but may lead to further investigation.

If there has been any situation in which there was a child in the household where there may have been alcohol misuse or drug use, you must explain the circumstances fully, including the steps you took to ensure the safeguarding of the child(ren). We will also need to speak to the other parent of any child affected to ensure that you took every possible step to protect the child(ren).

Her Shoes

That's it. As I lock the door I'm finally ending that whole sorry chapter. We couldn't have carried on like that. I just wish they'd let me put her shoes on when they took her away.

By the time they got here, Alice had calmed down. She was sitting quietly in her favourite wicker chair in the conservatory, drinking coffee (with nothing in it, I checked) and she might have been all right. But the blood on the kitchen roll wrapped round my hand caught their eye.

When they arrived, I was wearing my old glasses held together with Sellotape. My new ones were lying next to the kettle, all twisted with no lenses in them. The glass is all in the bin apart from the bit that got in my hand. That's what gave it away, the blood. The woman officer worked it out. I couldn't lie, could I? That doesn't get you anywhere. You have to face things.

'Yes, she did hit me,' I told them. 'Only once though, and the glasses fell off...'

The other one, the man, kept asking me things over and over, like he was Paxman or something, 'You haven't answered my question...' He asked why my hands were swollen. I've got a rash from the Christmas tree – an allergic reaction to the glue. Danny calls them my Incredible Hulk hands.

'Where did the blood come from?' the man asked. Then it was, 'Why did she stand on them?' and, 'I don't see how that could have been an accident.' He was so damned persistent. They seem determined to have someone to blame. Blame doesn't solve anything. Then he realised they've been here twice before. At one point they seemed to think I might have hit her. What kind of a man must they think I am?

I have to admit it was scary when my glasses came off. I couldn't see properly, and I was scrambling around on the floor, and she was screaming accusations at me. It's my own fault. I shouldn't have put my hand there. It wouldn't stop bleeding for ages but it didn't hurt. In an odd way it was a sort of relief. It's the first time in days I've not noticed the itching.

The glasses made a really loud crunching noise when she stamped on them. She deliberately picks things that make dramatic sounds; the chime of a metronome echoing around the body of my grand piano; a dinner plate smashed against a marble fireplace – much more satisfying than the tinkle of a wine glass. Not that we've got any wine glasses left. She drinks out of a mug these days, thinks I won't be able to tell how much she's had. But I keep a close eye on her, and I know most of her hiding places. Those half-bottles of vodka are only small, but with practice you can spot the red tops. I found four last week, one in the toilet cistern in the en-suite. I have a circuit that I do every night. It only takes about ten minutes if I've had a quick search during the day. My personal best is three in one night (inside a box of Sugar Puffs, gardening coat sleeve and the top shelf of Danny's toy cupboard).

Anyway, that's when I called the police, when my glasses got broken. I just panicked. You can't leave things like that – someone might get hurt. But I wish they had been a bit more patient and let me put her shoes on. She took them off when she went into the conservatory because of the glass stuck to the soles. She'd have gone to bed quietly if they had given her a bit more time: it was nearly midnight and she must have been tired. And she wouldn't need to get up tomorrow as I can look after Danny.

We have a nice routine, Danny and me. Routine is important for a child. I like things to be done in a certain order. That's why it's so difficult when she drinks. To be fair, it's not as bad as people think. I mean, some days she doesn't drink, a glass of wine maybe, but they reckon it's good for you, an odd glass. I've been to a couple of those Al-Anon meetings where the relatives of addicts meet. The people that go to those really are sad. They've simply accepted things for years. Step one: admit there's a problem.

Danny's fast asleep. He was as good as gold at bedtime. He wanted to watch *Chitty Chitty Bang Bang,* and I said he could stay up until the kids in the film went to bed. He went up without a battle. I sang him *Hushabye Mountain* as I tucked him in. Last time we watched it Alice cried because her childhood wasn't like that. Danny looked puzzled. He doesn't know about any of it.

They'll probably tell Social Services now, another bunch of interfering people. I bet they'll try and imply I had something to do with it and be all supportive to her, like she's the victim. Last time that counselling woman kept staring at the cut on Alice's forehead and frowning. She's always bruising herself.

What will happen to Danny?

She said she'll never let me see him again. She always says that when she's angry. I know she doesn't mean it; it's just the drink talking. She knows I'll always look after him. She even insisted that we made a will so that I'll look after Danny, not anyone else, if anything happens to her.

I really want a cigarette. She's smoked every last one. No wonder I get so bloody angry. She's sat here, smoking and drinking while I'm at the office all day. Then I have to look after Danny and clear up after her, and I can't even have a smoke, and my hands are killing me.

I suppose we'll have to sell the house now. It was meant to be our happy-ever-after house. I'll have to paint the dining room, cover those stains near the fireplace. That wedding photo needs dusting. She was beautiful in that dress. Danny loves it here, his space bedroom with all the planets, and the park behind the house. I've promised him we'll get some fish if he helps me clean the pond.

We had two carp last year, but a heron ate them. I heard it on the gravel and got as far as the conservatory door, but I thought better of it. I mean, have you seen the size of them? I didn't want to pick a fight with *that*.

I'd better get to bed, lots to do in the morning. Get rid of that bottle under the cushion in the conservatory. I'm pretty sure she's only got the one bottle on the go. Leave the window open, let some air in. I don't want it to be a mess when she gets back. She needs things to be as normal as possible. That's why I'm so good for her. I always keep things in order. Everyone says we should have some time apart, but she'll have to come back. I mean, where else is she going to go? Her mum won't have her after last time. Her stepdad, Lenny, was still angry when I picked her up.

I'll get up early and sort Danny out. He's got a party to go to on Sunday. His friend, Ben, will be five. I'll have to get a present and go to the opticians. We can go to McDonald's; Danny's collecting the Pooh characters. Then I'll pick her up. How else can she get home? She hasn't got any money, and she's got nothing on her feet. That's still bothering me. I tried to convince them she'd be all right at home but they insisted, something about a risk of a further breach of the peace. Further? Then she began to get upset again, and when the woman officer threatened to arrest her, she started to kick off…

'Never mind arresting me! What about whoever did that to your hair? That's who you should arrest, or did you cut it yourself, love?'

Then she tousled the policewoman's hair. That tore it. It all got a bit loud, and the other one tried to intervene. She gave him some words too.

'Ooh, look at the big man. Have you got a big truncheon, sweet-heart? Are you two a couple? You could do better than 'er. I mean, look at her *hair*. Bet I could teach you a thing or two…'

He said, 'I think we should all calm down.' Then she really warmed up.

'Don't you tell me to calm down...' followed by her old favourite, 'My eyes are up here.' It soon escalated to, 'Take your hands off me, you scrawny bitch...'

In the end they insisted she had to go with them. They said once they've been called they can't leave a situation. But she kept resisting and they called their mates with the van, said they couldn't be sure it was safe to take her in the car. But I mean, does it take four of you? She won't hurt anyone. All right, it has got to the stage of a bit of pushing and shoving once or twice. I only try to stop her from hitting me and pulling my hair. Anyway, they've taken her away now, no sense in going over all that again.

If they'd just let me put her shoes on. She was cutting her feet on the path when they were dragging her out. I was bending down trying to put her shoes on, my slippers kept falling off, but she wouldn't stay still, and that policewoman told me to get out of the way, bossy bitch.

They don't know what it was like for her. Her ex really was a violent man. That was proper hitting, and he is a big bloke too, Bill, taller than me. He never had to deal with the police. She was too scared to ring them. We met when she finally left him. Danny was still a baby, and she didn't want him growing up in a bad environment. Her grandad saw the black eyes and gave her some money before he died so she could get her own place. She didn't have a proper father figure growing up, so it hit her hard when she lost him. She sometimes talks about her grandad when she's had a few. Actually she talks *to* him quite a bit.

It was so romantic when we first met. My sister's friend, Mel, knew her from the salon and set us up. She hadn't exaggerated about her looks, and I was confident in those days. A baby would have completed things. It would have been nice for Danny to have a little brother or sister. But we never really talked about it after the miscarriage.

Anyway, I'm here to look after them both now. She forgets how good I am to her and Danny. I toilet-trained him all by myself – she's no patience – and I take him to school every day since she had her licence taken off her. And she says *I'm* a bastard. You should ask how *he* treated her.

There was one unfortunate incident when she fell and accidentally broke her ribs… one rib. All I was doing was putting her to bed. I pushed her so she'd land on the mattress but she accidentally landed on the wooden post at the end. You could hear it crack. She's put on quite a bit of weight since she stopped work. It was horrible, her breathing went all funny. She said, 'Oh, God, I've really hurt myself.' Then she started saying it was my fault and threatening me. But it was her fault… She did say 'hurt myself'. I took her straight down to A&E and stayed with her all night. Anyway, only one rib was cracked, and it's not that serious. She was all right after a couple of weeks.

Our neighbour, Sandra, looked after Danny that night. Her boy, Luke, is Danny's best friend, and she's often here, sharing a bottle of wine. Sandra understands the situation. I often have to speak to Sandra when Alice goes AWOL.

* * *

Danny is happy, dreaming in his bed with all his toys. Tigger's his favourite. I love that yellow glow from his night light, helps me see my way around when everyone's asleep. I bought it when he started to wake up in the night saying he could hear shouting and banging. I said it was probably the bin men, and the smashing noise must have been a cat or a fox knocking over a milk bottle.

And that picture of her twins over the stairs. Asleep.

I'll get up early and clean the kitchen floor before Danny stands on it. I need to have a quick once around and see if there are any new bottles.

I'll call Alice's mum in the morning. Last time Lenny threatened to come round and beat me up, like I'd done something wrong! I don't know what version of things she's been telling them.

I've got a blinding headache. And I'll have to go round in these stupid broken glasses for a few days. I liked my new glasses too.

I'll just wash my face, brush my teeth and get some sleep. I wish Sandra was here. I can talk to her, she'd understand. It's very unfair the things they say about her on the estate, she's coped very well since her husband left her. I might nip round tomorrow, let the boys play together.

I keep thinking about that time Sandra kissed me at New Year. The two of them were having a drink in the conservatory while I watched *E.T.* with the boys. I was in the kitchen getting some snacks. Sandra came right up to me and put her arms round me and... she kissed me full on the lips. She's finally got rid of that thug of a soldier she was seeing. She admitted she was impressed when he beat up Jack in the Crown, made a right mess of him. Anyway, she's single now.

Jesus, my eyes look old. I'm only thirty-seven. Better get a few hours' sleep. Hopefully she'll feel better too after a good sleep. I hope she's not cold at the police station. Her feet will be sore. I must remember to take her shoes when I go and get her. Oooh, the cold water's nice on my hands.

What the hell's that banging? At this time of night? They'll wake Danny. All right, I'm coming!

* * *

You'll never believe what's happened. That bastard, Bill, turned up. Had his brother with him too – he's another six-footer. I told him he couldn't come in, but what was I supposed to do? I don't want the police here again, and no one believes me. He bloody took Danny right out of his bed! There's no need for that. Everything's under control. Turns out Lenny had rung him. He's doing it out of spite. Whose side's he on? Danny was half-asleep, didn't know what was going on.

There's no way I'm letting that bastard keep Danny without a fight. His parents have been at war since he was born. The things they said about each other in court when Bill applied for residence! I can't see how Danny will be better off moving away and not seeing his mum or his friends.

I'll talk to her in the morning, and I'll get a solicitor on Monday. That Edie, who did our will, was nice. Maybe this will be the thing that finally sobers Alice up. They say that about a moment of clarity.

Her shoes are still sitting there. I bought them for her on our honeymoon in Jamaica. She liked that they were open-toed and she could easily slip them on, and the wooden platform soles made her an inch taller (but they bloody hurt when she kicked me). One of the flowers has come off the top.

My hands are killing me; I think there's still a bit of glass in there. What time is it? Twelve forty. Is it too late to call Sandra? I wonder if Luke's at his dad's this weekend. Danny always pretends he likes it at his dad's.

Right, I'll get everything sorted out in the morning then I'll give Sandra a call. Where's my mobile? I usually hide it in my suit pocket so she can't throw it. I haven't even got changed yet. I must stop hanging my jacket there at the bottom of the stairs – it'll get creased. Will I really call Sandra? I can't go round now, can I? What about my hands?

Where did I put the flower off that shoe? She said she'd sew it back on but she hasn't had time. It might be in her sewing basket on the top shelf…

Ha! Another half-bottle right at the back. Can't even tell it's there without stretching. She must have stood on a chair. Tip most of it out and top it up with water. If I take it away, she knows I've found it. This way, she'll have less. Worst thing is when she goes out looking for more at night. She's safer here with me. She'll stop now anyway. This will be the turning point.

Let's have a look for this flower first. Might be tricky sewing with my Incredible Hulk hands.

Ah-ha! There it is, the little green flower! I knew I'd kept it. I'll stitch it back on then she can wear them in the morning. There's no green cotton, only white. No one will notice. The important thing is that they are mended. Tricky to thread the needle with my fingers swollen… Ow! These glasses aren't ideal either.

The needle's eased the itch in my thumb. Try again. Break the surface, let the pressure out.

That's definitely relieving it. What was I doing…? I bet I can get that last bit of glass out from my palm with the needle. Break that bit where it's started to heal over.

Ooooh. Now it's bleeding. Sweet, or is it salty? Metallic. It's running all the way down to my wrist. If I wiggle that there…

Ah! That's got it. I'll keep this needle. That bit's starting to heal up again, give it another dig…

9.0 Identity, Diversity and Faith

How has the applicant's view of their own identity (personal, class, racial and ethnic, gender, sexual, cultural, language and spiritual etc.) and their attitude towards, and experience of, diversity influenced their views and plans about promoting an adoptive child's cultural heritage, racial identity and religious beliefs?

As an equal opportunities authority we encourage applications from people of all faiths, creeds and belief systems and we support applications from applicants who are gay, lesbian, heterosexual, bi-sexual or transsexual without discrimination. Children of many ethnicities and sometimes of mixed race may be approved for adoption. Complete the Equal Opportunities Monitoring (form EOMF/98/1001). Consider how you feel about your own racial identity and how you would support an adopted child(ren) in understanding his or her own identity.

Were you raised with a religious faith? If so, how does that influence the choices you might make when supporting a child? It may be that a child has been raised within a specific faith and that it is their wish, or that of their birth parents, that they continue to practise that faith. How would you support that, and how would you educate a child to understand a culture of diversity and tolerance?

Think about how religion has affected your own family. How does that inform your own values about faith? It may not necessarily be a barrier to approval if you have any religious preferences, but if you express any strong conviction for a faith it may reduce the opportunities for adoption or lead to a longer period before matching (subject to approval).

9.1 Equal Opportunities Form for monitoring purposes

We are committed to the successful development of an equal opportunities policy in all aspects of our work. To assist in the implementation and monitoring of this policy, we request that everyone participating in any of our programmes and services provide the information below.

This information will not affect the outcome of your application or interactions with the relevant deparment, and the information you provide will be treated in the strictest confidence.

1. I describe my race or ethnic group as:

South Asian / Asian British		Mixed	
Indian		White and East Asian	
Pakistani		White and Black Caribbean	
Bangladeshi		White and Black African	
Other South Asian		Other mixed	
Black / Black British		**White**	
Caribbean		British	
African		Irish	
Other Black		Other white	
East Asian		**Other**	
Chinese		Please specify	
Other East Asian			

2. My gender is:

Male ☐   Female ☐   Other / prefer not to say ☐

3. My sexual orientation is:

Straight ☐   Gay ☐   Other / prefer not to say ☐

4. Do you have a disability?

Yes ☐   No ☐   Are you registered disabled? ☐

5. My age is:

16–19 ☐   20–29 ☐   30–39 ☐   40–49 ☐   50–59 ☐   60+ ☐

Veritas Nunquam Perit, Part II:
Our Lady's Toes

You are sitting outside the headmaster's office. Above you, look-ing down from heaven, are portraits of three headmasters, all in black. You have an odd thought looking at the gothic frames and the dark eyes of these men: in the film of this story these characters would be played by Peter Cushing, Boris Karloff and Christopher Lee. You think about the film you were allowed to stay up and watch recently, classified 'not suitable' by your mother – *The Wicker Man*. It was the first time you had seen a naked woman on screen. Your dad had a cushion on his lap. You think of Britt Ekland's pubic triangle, her breasts. Another erec-tion is about to be born, your third today. You try to suppress it and look around to check there is no one coming. The cor-ridor is deserted. No one is malingering – a serious crime – or, worse still, running. You have already started to have a recurring nightmare about hurrying along these corridors. The dream will stay with you well into your career.

Your feet are itchy, and you are sweaty all over from play-ing twenty-a-side football on the playground with a tennis ball. Football is not allowed. Rugby is the official sport.

You feel the portraits staring at you. One of the Brothers will die in a fire when he is away on retreat in France two years from now. Your mother will insist that you pray for him, and there will be even more Latin masses than usual. Will he have screamed 'Oh my God!' like the devout Christian policeman in *The Wicker Man*?

Brother Kelly, the last headmaster on the wall, was nicknamed Frankenstein because of his large square head. He stopped you in the corridor once and asked your name. Then he said, 'Extraordinary eyes.' You still don't know why that felt odd. You told your mother. She looked away and quoted your grandma. '"He'll break some hearts with them eyes." That's what my mum always said.' Then she blew her nose because her mother had died only days before your last sister was born at Easter. All the will of God, your mother tells you.

A coat of arms boasts the school's motto in Latin: *Veritas Nunquam Perit.* You do quite well in Latin, so you know it could be translated as, 'Truth Never Perishes', or, better, 'Truth Never Dies'. Saint Peter is quoted under a black and white picture of Blessed Ernest Whittle. He has something to do with founding the school. The quote says, *Silence is the greatest sin.* What would you say if you were asked about some of the things you'd seen in the classroom? What are you going to do when you hear about a court case thirty-five years from now?

The headmaster's door creaks open. You feel cold. You've never been in there before. You aren't here for a disciplinary reason – which is why boys are usually sent for – but because you have been singled out by Mr Austin, the deputy head teacher. The nominal head, Brother Brady, is as old as a mummy and is never seen. Another boy from your class was sent for recently. His dad was a famous footballer. He doesn't join in the tennis-ball football anymore.

'Come in, my boy. Accept my apologies for keeping you waiting,' he says in educated tones that echo with authority. Bach is playing sotto voce in the background. You will never again be able to listen to Bach without feeling a physical reaction to its measured counterpoint. You will stop playing the piano soon, partly because there's always a Bach piece in the exam and you won't even be able to listen to Bach anymore.

He looks down on you and smiles.

'Don't be afraid.'

You don't know whether to smile back, so you go halfway and feel idiotic. You feel your cheeks warming. You are too old to blush, you think, but it happens often at school.

A giant arm guides you into the office and you wonder how tall Mr Austin must be. You are as tall as most in your class but you scarcely reach his chest. He is wearing a large black cloak, earned because he is a Reverend. He reminds you of Bela Lugosi.

You are steered to a leather armchair opposite a grand baroque desk. He takes his place on a throne behind the desk. Jesus looks down sadly from a heavy crucifix above you. You try and remember what the acronym *INRI* on the scroll above His head stands for. A bluebottle hurries around on the blood that stains His crown of thorns. You have to fight an urge to scratch your greasy hair.

Mr Austin flicks through a file, making noises of approval. He asks you about your piano lessons and your academic performance. You have made good progress in your third year at the school. Your answers are monosyllabic.

Through the arched window you spot a crow silently land in the old oak tree on the school drive.

He wants to know if there is anything that concerns you. You know you aren't going to say anything about what you saw in the changing rooms after games last week. Are you supposed to tell someone about that? What would happen to you if you did?

An ivory statue of the Virgin Mary prays serenely for you on the opposite wall, arms open, palms up. She is crushing a serpent beneath her bare feet. Later you will notice her toes. You will be able to describe those toes in incredible detail far into the future. Whenever your mother brings you a picture of Our Lady when she returns from retreat, you will always check the toes.

He asks you why you aren't a soloist in the choir. You make a modest comment about not being good enough, but you are lying: that's not the reason. Lying is a venial sin, not a mortal one, but you'll have to confess it. Normally at confession you only have immoral thoughts to confess – four times last week.

The music changes from a plodding prelude to an allegro fugue in a minor key as Mr Austin lowers himself onto the edge of the desk immediately in front of you. His voice has become softer, almost a whisper.

'I'd like to take you into a confidence that I keep for certain exceptional boys. I have a gift for you, and I was hoping that you and I could become close, rather like a special parental relationship. I will do everything in my power to help you.'

You have no idea what this means, so you gaze up at him without making actual eye contact. 'Yes, sir.' A crucifix on a silver chain dangles from his neck. That would ward off vampires, you think.

'I'd like us to have a personal understanding. I want you to promise that anything that is said or takes place here will never leave this room. Do you understand?'

You don't quite follow but you say, 'Yes, sir,' again anyway. His hair has a widow's peak.

'Good. Then we understand one another. Now we're going to have a little chat about God's gifts, and let's see where that leads us.'

'Yes, sir.'

'"As each has received a gift, use it to serve one another, as good stewards of God's varied grace,"' he quotes. 'Do you know where that's from?'

'Is it Saint Peter, sir?'

'Excellent! It is indeed. Peter 4:10.'

You decide against telling him that Peter is your confirmation name as well as that of the school.

'Now then...' He reaches a monstrous arm behind himself to where a square white box is sitting on the desk. His enormous hand clutches the box like the robotic claws of the remote-controlled crane that fails to pick up prizes in the arcades at Blackpool. His arm scythes through 180 degrees until the box is immediately in front of you. This will be the first of several visits here, though not all will result in gifts. 'Go on, son. It's a gift for you, a reward. I want you to be one of my special boys.' He smiles again. 'I'd like us to meet here from time to time. This will be our private time together.'

You know by now that something is badly wrong with this conversation, but you are unable to understand what. The white box is a few inches from your face, and his black frame blocks out everything else. You feel a powerful hand on your shoulder as you take the box in both hands with a meek, 'Thank you, sir.'

Once you have opened this box, you will have unwittingly entered into a contract of sorts. You will still be thinking about that far into the next century.

In a moment you are going to feel your cheek pressed hard against the desk. Something sharp will dig into your ear and you won't be able to move. You will be inhaling furniture polish, looking at Our Lady's feet. The serpent is trapped, choking. You will always feel sick at the smell of furniture polish. You will hear his voice, but you won't be able to make out any words or produce any of your own. Her toenails are short, and there is dirt between her toes, like the athlete's foot with which you are afflicted. He is going to roughly tug down your trousers and your white St Michael Y-fronts. He will press down on your back. There is a chip on her left little toe showing the white beneath. You will feel something cold and slimy being rubbed into your anus. What is the statue made of, you'll wonder. He will grunt as he pushes and shoves and tries to force himself inside you. Ten toes... ten Hail Marys... Hail

Mary, full of grace… He can't quite manage it and seems to be getting angry. You will hear him behind you, his breath becoming more and more hoarse. He will moan, 'My God! Christ! Jesus!' It will remind you of the end of *The Wicker Man*. You will feel a warm wet splat on your buttocks.

'Open the box, my boy,' he will say. 'Go on, open it.'

You open the box.

10.0 Health and Safety, Criminal Records and Statutory Checks

Please complete the Health and Safety Risk Assessment forms on the following pages. Make sure you complete every section. You will need to arrange a visit from your local fire station to assess any potential fire risks and to make sure that suitable smoke and carbon monoxide alarms are installed throughout the property. Your attention is drawn to your statutory obligations regarding safety. If any potential hazards are identified such as water in any garden or potential hazardous substances an inspector from the Council's Health and Safety Directorate will carry out an inspection and make recommendations for remedial measures. If you are instructed to carry out any works for safety reasons these will need to be completed before you can be recommended tor approval.

Each applicant must carry out a DBS check. Once you have completed a DBS check, your social worker will address any issues arising. The DBS check will need to be renewed annually for as long as you are in the process. A DBS check for any other purpose, such as employment or work with children, will not suffice.

If you have ever been on the Violent and Sex Offender Register (ViSOR), you are excluded from the adoption process.

If any member of your family or wider social network has ever been investigated or cautioned for any related offence, whatever the outcome, you are required to give full details. It is your responsibility to have made enquiries about this.

For other crimes it is not necessarily the case that you will be excluded from the process, especially if convictions were a long time ago. In most cases minor driving offences, apart from drink driving, will not be considered to affect the application process. However, you are reminded that you must state clearly if you have ever been convicted of any crime or cautioned by the police. It is especially important to declare any issue relating to drugs or alcohol-related crime and any violent crime, however minor and however long ago.

Explain here the details of any spent convictions or other relevant matter.

Health & Safety Risk Assessment (cont)	Checked (initials)	Not Present	Notes *Further Guidance Work Required
Item 7.2 External			
Driveway Clear, even surface, no trip hazards			
Parking, safe access, barrier to footpath / road			*Gate to public highway*
Lock on gates and suitable safe fencing			*Must be child-proof for whole perimeter of property*
Safe storage of power tools, tools equipment			
Garages, sheds, gazebos, summer houses Trampolines, swings, and other high-risk items			*Must be kept locked Check all glass*
Flammable items inc. fuel (see COSHH regulations and procedures)			***COSHH assessment for all potentially hazardous materials***
Steps and hard paved areas / trip hazards			
Sandpits, flower beds, pots and containers			
Compost areas			
Sharp / poisonous plants			*No more than 8 high-risk plants*
Drain covers, surface water drainage			
Ponds, water features, water tanks, pools			*Must be behind fencing /barrier, including natural ponds*
Beehives, birds' nests, other animals			
Safe area/ proves for animal waste (pets)			
Chemicals – weed killer, insect poisons etc.			*Locked indoors on high shelf*
Machinery e.g. mowers, strimmers and other power tools			*Must be securely locked inside*
External water supply, hoses, taps			
External plugs, lighting / electrical			*To be tested to current guidance*
Item 7.3 Fire Safety			
Inspection by Fire Service completed			
Smoke Alarms tested			*Must comply with current RS, mains connected, min one alarm per floor*
Fire extinguisher / fire blanket present			

(Continued)

My Knee

My knee hurts quite badly. It's all flooding back now, the way the pain starts when you stub your toe. You know it's coming but there's a pause before it bites.

Pippa and I had been out for dinner at the French, a sort of truce. We'd been civilised all evening, given the circumstances, and had managed to eat without arguing. Good wine always helps. I still had my grey suit on, and she wore a tight-fitting black skirt. She's been dressing smarter for work this year, always wears lipstick. We kept the conversation to siblings and work. We didn't talk about the situation at all.

An evening of calm before the impending crisis, that's what we'd agreed. I'd done a good job of keeping things sensible for the last month while she sorted herself out. But something was bound to happen with Pippa around.

We were almost back at the house (I suppose I should start calling it *my* house). I'd won the argument that she'd drive. It was only fair I had a drink after what she'd done, and she was still feeling guilty, so she wouldn't argue. Besides, I didn't like being in my car with her after that time she borrowed it one Sunday, 'to meet some German visitors at the airport', with her boss. His Merc only has two seats. Her Mini was too small.

We were about to cross the hump-backed bridge at the end of our street… *my* street. This is where Pippa announced, 'I could live round here!' when we first came to look at houses in this area four years ago. Then the it happened.

A car came *flying* over the bridge. None of the wheels were touching the road. I felt a surge of adrenalin. It was like someone had their finger on freeze frame. Like the night I first found out.

Approval

Pippa let go of the steering wheel, covered her face and screamed. The other car squealed and hit us with a thump. It made a vicious noise; screeching, smashing, crunching; an oddly exhilarating moment. Then a prolonged hiss and the news still playing on the car radio.

A woman was stabbed repeatedly...

Was she all right? The seatbelt had tugged at my chest but I was fine. I could see Pippa wasn't hurt, but she was hysterical. 'My Mini!' she said. 'She's killed my Mini!' The windscreen had been smashed to an opaque mosaic.

...pronounced dead at the scene.

The other driver, another young woman, was already out of her car and was staring at the wreckage.

...officer said, 'This was a sustained and frenzied attack.'

I turned the radio off.

'Are you all right?' I asked Pippa. I put my hand on hers. She pulled it away and rummaged for her phone. The phone I bought her last Christmas.

'I'm all right, but look at the state of my car!'

I reached over, turned the ignition off and took the key out.

My car? Strictly speaking, it should go down as a marital asset. The Audi is a company car, so technically the Mini was *our* car. And I'd paid for it last year with my bonus, back when business was good. My solicitor said it was best to list that kind of thing in case hers started getting funny about pensions and such. I told him I didn't want any conflict. It's always better to avoid conflict.

I unfastened the seatbelt.

I hadn't even been angry at Pippa when I first found out. I'd nipped out for a quick pint at the Griffin, and I saw the Mini snuggled up to his flashy Merc. Vince, her boss.

I swung the door open and got out of the car.

An Ann Summers party in Bury, she'd told me. Please show

me a *bit* of respect. When she came clattering in about midnight, I challenged her. She hadn't even bought anything. People always buy something, don't they? And what would she need that kind of thing for anyway? She had too much lipstick on.

The wind slapped my face.

First thing she did when I confronted her with my clues was to laugh. She said it was a nervous laugh. I poured her the last of the wine and opened another bottle, and we sat and talked at the kitchen table. She didn't say anything about me drinking for once. She confessed what she'd done in my car. She said she hoped I could find a way to forgive her. I said there's no point in getting angry.

There was a whiff of petrol and smoke in the air.

Before I could get round to the mangled front of the Mini the other woman had started shouting at Pippa through the window, pointing her blood-red fingernails and wagging her shaggy blonde hair. What was she shouting about? It wasn't Pippa's fault. The woman had on those black leggings that Pippa always wears – they didn't look as good on her.

I could smell burning rubber.

'What the hell were you doing?' The woman had a Manchester accent.

There's no need to shout like that.

Now Pippa was out and squaring up to her. 'You've smashed my bloody car in, you stupid cow!' When she was angry she lapsed into a Suffolk accent that sounded more Essex than her usual how-now-brown-cow. It was the same when she cried. There'd been a lot of that recently. She kept asking what was going to happen to her. I've been more than fair about the house and the money after what she's done to me.

The other woman was grabbing her. 'Who are you calling a cow?'

I stepped between them before things got out of hand. I've had plenty of practice calming people down recently: Dougie, when he told me to kick her out; and Pippa's mum, Bunny, she got all teary too. I'm the one that loses half my family. I'll probably never see them again. Now I might never have a family of my own. If I can keep control, why can't everyone else?

'Calm down,' I said. 'There's no need to get excited...'

'What it got to do with you?' Now the woman was rearing up at me. 'You stink of booze!'

You can only push me so far.

Pippa stepped forward again. 'What's that got to do with anything?'

'Has she been drinking too?'

'It's your fault, you were going too fast!' Pippa said.

'Look, let's all stay calm and get this sorted out,' I said. 'Is anyone hurt?'

The woman said, 'I'm not hurt, but look at the state of my car. You'll have to pay for it!'

Pippa started crying, bent over the Mini's gnarled wheel arch. I put my arm around her. She shrugged it off.

'It'll be all right,' I said. 'We'll get the insurance sorted, and everything will be all right.'

'Yeah! I want your insurance,' the woman said.

'You were on the wrong side of the road,' I said, quietly but firmly.

'So were you!'

'No, I wasn't,' Pippa cried. 'Look where the cars are!'

The Mini was kissing the kerb, its cute face ruined. The other car, a dirty black Golf, was slewn diagonally across the centre line, the front embedded in the Mini. Pippa's bumper had come off altogether, the blue bonnet was twisted out of shape. The headlights were smashed.

'That's where you swerved!'

I raised my arms to show everyone to simmer down. Even when Pippa got upset about furniture and having to find a new flat, I was in control. Someone has to be rational.

'Let's swap insurance details and wait till the police get here,' I said.

'What do you want the police for?' the woman screamed. 'It's not my fault. It's that road!'

'Actually, there have been a few accidents here,' I said. I wondered why she was being so aggressive... defensive, really. It is a known accident spot. You can't see who's coming from the opposite direction.

Pippa was clutching her phone to her ear. Did she have to call? Now?

Some idiot beeped their horn. For Christ's sake!

By now there were cars stopped on both sides of the bridge. The man that lives three doors down, BMW driver, personal injury solicitor, was directing traffic and telling everyone what had happened.

'Is everyone all right? May I help, I'm a solicitor.'

Show-off! It's like that at work: Michael, the FD, he's another, pointing out people's mistakes.

'I don't think anyone's injured,' I said.

Show-off spoke to the other woman then he went over and put his greedy arm round Pippa's shoulder. Why's it always about her? She'd gone round there to sit with his girlfriend a couple of times over the last month. It's hard enough without involving anyone else. I hadn't even shouted at her. I was letting her have all the best crockery and glasses (I'd typed a list). I'd have preferred it if people left us alone. First that smug pair sticking their noses in, now this.

It started spitting.

The woman was examining her car, it looked like she was going to start blubbing too. She was muttering under her breath.

It was after ten and I had to get ready for the Friday Fright (our weekly roasting from the boss) before I could go bed. The last couple of meetings hadn't gone very well. I've had a lot on my mind. Now I was going to have to deal with all this as well tomorrow. I was planning a nightcap, so I could sleep.

The rain was now hissing on the damaged cars.

'What's your name?' I asked, taking a pen from my lapel pocket and looking at her number plate.

'What's yours?' she sneered. 'Who put you in charge, you lanky get?'

I looked at Pippa. She might have laughed at that in better circumstances. She was talking softly on the mobile now, glancing at me.

There was a nasty burning taste in the air.

'Listen, it's simply a matter of getting all the insurance…'

'…simply a matter of ner-ner-ner…' The woman was doing the sneery mimic that Pippa did when we used to argue. Only when Pippa did it, it didn't mean anything, they weren't serious arguments.

The rain was stinging my face.

It's not just a fling.

That's what Pippa said that night, as if somehow a fling would be all right. I can still see her lipstick smeared on the wine glass.

A siren cried in the distance.

The woman stood there, shouting at me, stabbing her finger. There's no need for that. Even though we had to deal with challenging circumstances, Pippa and I always kept things polite. Pippa was busy on the phone now with her back to me.

I wanted to fling that phone away.

The rain was getting harder.

The woman had her hands on her fat hips, spitting filthy words from her bloody red lips.

Too much lipstick.

I couldn't hear what she was saying.

I couldn't hear Pippa either.

The rain was pecking at my brain. My ears were throbbing. My face was burning. I could taste acid.

Not.

Just.

A fling.

Everything stayed still. It was as if I was watching it happen.

I stepped towards the woman with my arm out and she slapped me away with her hand. I grabbed hold of her coat. She pushed my arm quite hard and caught me off balance. I slipped over. That's when I banged my knee on the kerb. It really hurt, like it used to when you fell over in the playground. I got up and pushed her back. She fell backwards in slow motion. It took ages for her to fall. She didn't put her hands out. Her skull cracked with a clunk on the kerb. Blood burst from her gob as the bone bounced off the concrete.

Pippa screamed.

After that it went very quiet. It's quiet now and I feel calm, but my knee hurts.

11.0 Data Protection and Privacy

11.1.1 Privacy Statement

It is vitally important that the Council's confidential records are kept confidential. Please carefully read the Privacy Statement and the Confidentiality and Non-disclosure forms (Forms EO 2003/1012 and Form EO 2003/968) and sign and date them. If you are applying as a couple, you must both sign both documents.

You are reminded that any matter relating to the welfare of a child must be subject to the most stringent confidentiality. The Council is striving to protect the rights of all of its citizens, including adopted children and birth parents of adopted children. You must be able to demonstrate that you have understood the need for protection of privacy, as per your training in the Fostering and Adoption Training and Development Programme, and your social worker will discuss this fully with you.

11.1.2 Data Protection Act 1998

Under the Data Protection Act 1998 you are entitled to request a copy of any data about you that is held by the Council. In order to access any information you may make a written 'Subject Access Request'. You are only allowed to access data about yourself. Your request must include your full name and address and a copy of proof of identity. Acceptable forms of identification include a passport or your driving licence. You should include as much information as possible in your request as this will facilitate us being able to access your information in the quickest time possible. We will respond to any Subject Access Requests within 40 calendar days.

For more information about the Council's privacy policy and the Data Protection Act, refer to the Prospective Adopters Information Pack or the Council's website.

B

It all started with a tweet. I'd no idea it would get as big as it did. And it's certainly not fair what happened to me, regardless of what you think of him.

It was one of those idle Tuesday afternoons. I'd only left work at the old place a year ago and I was writing and blogging. The Internet was full of rumours about celebrity scandals – who'd done this, who's done that – and I remembered my old piano teacher Pete. Pete the Piano, I used to call him. I wondered how he'd been taking all of this Jimmy Savile/Rolf Harris/Stuart Hall speculation. Anyway, it was about ten years ago when Pete used to tell me showbiz gossip from when he worked at the BBC. Pete was gay, said he knew a big secret.

I was at the laptop thinking about stories. I tweeted to see what would happen. I have this rule where I try and use exactly 140 characters:

> You think they've caught them all? Savile, Rolf,
> Stuart Hall. I've got news. The biggest fish of
> all is yet to be exposed. Watch this space.

I was only trying to build up my own following. No such thing as bad publicity. I thought it might help with finding blog-writing work.

I got hundreds of replies, lots of them guesses. I made a point of replying 'No' to as many as I could (admittedly breaking my own 140-character rule, but you have to be flexible). That led to even more hits. I'd been tweeting for about six months, and I had about five hundred followers. Within three days, I was past two thousand. Then people started re-tweeting and it started trending and went up to eight thousand. In the end I got scared it was getting out of hand. I tweeted again (using the full 140):

> Thanks for all the tweets about the Big Fish.
> You can stop guessing now. I am not going to
> tell you who he is. I have to protect my sources.

It seemed to calm down for a few days after that. Then it came to my weekly beer night with Dougie, a tradition we'd kept up for years and years.

'So, you're telling me you know who the big fish is and you've a witness that was there at the time, like?'

'That's what I was told.'

'That's evidence, that is. You've got to report him. I mean, what if it's true? You've got a moral duty.'

'What if it isn't true?'

'I thought you said it was.'

'No, I said I knew a guy who speculated about it before all this stuff came out about Jimmy Savile.'

'It's your round.'

'Same?'

At the bar, my mind wandered. I thought of a clip I'd watched earlier on the Internet involving two Thai girls. I tried to count the beer mats in frames on the wall instead.

'Five eighty.'

I gave the barmaid six pound coins and a grin. 'Keep the change.'

'You must be feeling flush,' she said. 'Made your first million, have you?'

'This time next year…'

Dougie and I often speculated about who was going to write

the bestseller, be first on TV, write that Oscar-winning screenplay.

'Anyway, I reckon you've got to put it out there,' he said.

'It's not fair if I name him and it turns out he's innocent.'

'If he's innocent, he'll be exonerated.' He took a huge gulp of beer.

'What about my reputation?' I said.

'What reputation? This can only do you good.'

'How come?'

'Think of the coverage. How many of that book have they sold, the one where you wrote the foreword?'

'Few hundred, I think.'

'So, how helpful would it be if your name was associated with front-page news?'

I tried to calculate some numbers while he smiled. 'What if the police come and interrogate me?'

'This is the BBC we're talking about, not the Gestapo.'

'What if I get sued?'

'Then that's your next story. Sell that to the papers an' all. Remember, you'll be a famous writer by then. Controversial author...'

That made me smile. 'But what if they investigate me?'

'Who are they? The state-controlled-media-police? GCHQ? The FBI? You've seen too many fillums.'

'There's only one syllable in "film".'

'Beg your pardon, Mr Critic.'

We sat quietly for a moment. Here in the Gaunt, I felt safe. Of course I was being paranoid.

'Anyway, never mind the Daily Mail. You've got to tell me.' Dougie pointed a stubby finger at me.

'Why's that?'

'Because we share every secret. It's a rule, like.'

'We have rules?'

'I told you about that bird in the office. '

'You told me you had a fantasy! You never even did anything.'

'Same thing.'

We went on like this for a while but he wouldn't let it lie. In a way, I suppose I wanted to tell someone. You know that feeling when you've got a secret; you have to tell at least one person. Eventually I agreed to give him one letter. He can be persuasive, Dougie, when you've had four pints.

'B,' I said.

He smiled and frowned in an exaggerated way all at once. 'B, eh? Alreet, tell me again what your mate said, the piano man.'

'He said that when he worked at the studio in London on that show…'

'Which show?'

'You know, that one where they have dancing and singing and all that.'

'Puts a new meaning on the name of that programme…'

'Listen, that's not the point, the point is, B was all over the runners, teenage boys.'

'Not girls?'

'No, Pete said he was like one of those fluffer horses, rearing up, horny as hell, prancing around them he was.'

Dougie smiled and took a gulp of beer. 'Alreet then, way I see it, you have a duty to them poor kids.'

'I can't prove he did anything.'

'Doesn't mean he didn't.' He raised his eyebrows. 'Did your fella – Pete, was it? – get involved himself?'

'No, I don't think Pete was into older guys from the stories he told me, and by then B would have been no spring chicken.'

'How old is he now?'

'Nice try.'

'I'll get it out of you.'

'Besides, Pete would have been in his late twenties, bit old for

B's taste. He was a good-looking lad, mind.'

'You're not…?'

'Careful.'

'Anyhow, you can't keep calling him "B". Dougie did that infuriating *66–99* thing with his fingers.

'Why not?'

''Cos if you do, I'm gonna sit here all night and speculate about every celebrity whose name begins with B till you're sick of it. I'll include all your favourites. Listen… B███████, he's a B.'

'Not the right age though, is he?'

'Alreet, B██ C███████? B███ B████?

I attempted an impersonation of B███ C███████. Dougie looked bewildered.

'Where was I? B████ B██? B██ B   ? B██ O███?' He looked at me with each name, pretending to be watching my body language.

I shook my head. 'Bigger.'

'B█████ R██████?'

'He's dead.'

'God rest him. B████ R██████?'

'Too young.'

'B████ E█████? B██ I██?'

'No.'

'How about… B████ H████████?'

'Curiouser and curiouser, but nowhere near.'

'I know: B█████ H█… eh?'

I shook my head.

'B█████ D███████ …'

'Is he the one that does those antiques programmes?'

'Nah, you cock. The rock legend!'

'Not him anyway.'

Talking of rock legends, what about 'B████ S███████?'

'He's American!'

'So's B█ C█████ – he's a B, and he got convicted. Who else? B█████ F████?'

I sang a word of his most famous song.

'Y'nah, it's almost as if he was in the room. I know... B██ M█████████?' He attempted an impersonation with his eyebrows.

'Eh-uh!' I did the noise from the quiz show as accurately as I could.

An old man sipping a pint on the next table looked over.

'I can do this all neet,' Dougie said.

My beer was almost empty, and he would have gone on till he got there. I leaned forward. 'You have to promise me on all that is sacred that you will never tell a soul.'

'Scout's honour.' He did a thing with his fingers like something out of Star Trek.

'You weren't even in the Scouts.'

'Alreet, cross my heart...' He drew a rough cross on his chest with two fingers.

So I told him.

* * *

Up to this point nothing had happened; mate knows a name that someone once speculated about. But the idea had hold of me. I don't know why I did what I did next. I just felt compelled to do it. This time, contrary to my normal rule, I posted a very short tweet. I typed his first name.

One word. That's all it took. What I didn't know was that the forces of fate were about to take over. You see, Dougie knew some guy from work who knew a journalist. Anyway, this freelance journalist gave Dougie a few quid to spill the beans. He protested afterwards that he was under duress, but for pity's sake, you don't just cave in! I've known Dougie all our adult lives, and we've play-fully wound each other up. But what a bastard! Selling my secret to the press!

What neither of us realised was that me tweeting it, and him saying it, added up to two sources. I know what you think – jour-nalists don't follow strict ethical rules – but editors like to know a source. Well, their second source – 'Deep Throat', as I now call him – led to the whole thing blowing up.

But Dougie wasn't the one that got journalists turning up at his house. How did they know where I lived? They simply drove up my drive. One of them parked on the lawn. That's private prop-erty! They wouldn't go away, and I had to hide all evening, and I kept thinking about what would happen if they started to inves-tigate me. Not that I have anything to hide. I mean, there are a couple of stories from football trips before I met Cici, but they're subject to tour rules. And I would never do anything with a teen-age girl at my age even if she was…

What are you meant to do when journalists hassle you? Call your lawyer? Not that I had a lawyer, only the firm that dealt with the divorce and this was a bit out of their field.

After that I had a call from the police asking all sorts of questions.

Then Cici got all upset. I had to explain that it wasn't me they were investigating. Then I thought they might be after me. I bet it's because of his royal connections, with the OBE or Knighthood or whatever he has… had. What if one of those websites had… you know, the wrong kind of porn?

I spent most of that evening pacing up and down in the garden smoking, rehearsing what I was going to say when I got to the right authority. Then the police actually turned up at midnight saying a neighbour had called because they'd seen someone lurking in our garden. It'll be that nosy pair at number 37. That's an invasion of privacy.

That week was hard work-wise. I had to phone my client and ask for an extension. I went to one of those old-school Internet cafés. I should have done that in the first place, made up a name. But then I didn't realise you could commit a crime by tweeting. What happened to freedom of speech?

All I'd done was to tweet a name. Could have been anyone. Think of all the celebrities with that first name. Okay, maybe none quite so long-established: he is top of the page on Google when you type the first three letters.

What if there was a cover-up? Which would be better if you were the head honcho? One slightly known writer locked up on some trumped-up charge, or another huge scandal costing millions and discrediting the BBC? It had only been a few months since Savile. They couldn't afford another cock-up of that magnitude. And, as you know, B is one of the few celebs on TV who's that famous. Think about it, who's big enough to rival him? Simon Cowell, maybe?

Funny thing is, I remember Pete telling me about it with absolute conviction: 'You watch,' he said. 'When he dies, it will all come out.' Prophetic, Pete.

When I saw the headlines the next day I realised the magnitude of it. The tabloids really went to town on him. Some of the journalists had done plays on words about that quiz show he used to do. The people that appeared on that must be embarrassed. The Sun's headlines were in really bad taste. But the ones that were tweeted about most were a picture of a boy of about fourteen being chased around with B's grinning face stuck onto someone else's body beneath his catchphrase. They'd found some really lecherous-looking shots of him too. When you look at him closely in the light of what's been going on, he does have that look about him…

Then the victims appeared. One or two at first, then the flood-gates opened. Within a fortnight there were nearly fifty. Some of the allegations were decades old. They were my age. Surely they can't all have been victims. I mean, when did he have time to be on telly so much, and why did none of them say anything before? I suppose if that did happen, you'd want to try and forget it. It's not easy to say it out loud. One of them was a lad who committed suicide in 1986. His mum said she never knew the reason but now it all made sense. It made me think again about school. No one ever said anything in those days. We were all at risk in the Seventies.

I suppose you have to feel a bit sorry for him. I mean, bearing in mind the idea of innocent until proved guilty. He entertained generations of families and his life ended in disgrace.

Was it brave of him to end it? Did he have a choice? There were even suggestions of a Princess Di-style conspiracy: that he'd been bumped off because of his royal links. You've got to watch out. There's some nonsense on the Internet.

Not a good way to go though, hanging himself in a hotel room. Alone. Disgraced. I thought for a long time whether it was guilt that caused him to do it or whether it was the shame of watching his reputation being ruined. He should have been allowed a proper trial.

I got some nasty emails and tweets, like it was my fault. I even had my own troll. I refused to read the jokes in the weeks that followed – that's sick. I even felt a bit sad, another slice of my childhood memories corrupted. I mean, they've ruined my memories of Rolf Harris – all those jokes about Jake the Peg and didgeridoos. The whole family used to watch the programmes together – everyone did. My mum would never have let us even speak about it. In those days it was never said. That was half the problem at my school. No one said anything for years.

But the stories must have been true. There are too many victims. He obviously did everything in his power to take advantage of them. In the end these things have to come out, same as it did at St Peter's. It's hard to face that kind of thing, even years later.

The way I see it, I've helped a lot of innocent people. They'll get a fortune from his estate, those families. I suppose that's the name of the game. Given what has been done to them, they deserve it. It can hang around in your mind for years. In the end no one suffered from what I did, apart from B, and he was, you know...

I'll admit it did increase my following. The story about it sold well as fiction, which of course it isn't. Then I was in the papers a few times, and I got to meet M███████. By the way, did you know she did a sex video? You can look it up on YouTube. Just type 'M██████ sex video' on Google.

That's probably why the police showed an interest in me. I definitely didn't look at those kinds of pictures. I make sure I delete my browsing history, so Cici doesn't know about it. She kept going on about the websites, so I have to be careful.

I eventually forgave Dougie Deep Throat. His book comes out at Christmas. It's that cheap kind of soft porn for women – you know, the fifty shades of shit variety.

Anyway, my conscience is clear. Victims from my generation should get justice. I haven't done anything wrong. People like that should be locked up. And there can be no doubt about B's guilt now, can there?

12.0 Approval

The main body of the report is almost complete. This is your opportunity to say anything else that you may feel is relevant to your application. Is there anything that you don't feel was properly covered in your earlier answers about childhood or personal experiences that you would like to explain further? This might help you when you are completing the last section about matching criteria.

Go back through the draft report so far. Think about what that tells you about your past experiences and how that influences who you are and how you feel about being a parent. Think about how another person would describe you. Have you been completely honest?

You must also feel free to talk to your social worker about any other issues that concern you. It is important not to have any secrets.

This is also a final opportunity to consider what approval and adoption means to your life and to look back again at your motivations.

Veritas Nunquam Perit, Part III:
After the Trial

Mr Austin wasn't handcuffed, but his arm didn't move as I held out my hand. I am as tall as him now. I remember him towering over me in the sixth form, though I must have been six feet tall. He was sixty-five at the trial, so he would have been a young man when he taught me. I was finally going to confront him.

'Shaking hands isn't allowed, I'm afraid,' Mr Austin said. 'No physical contact.'

You wouldn't normally shake hands with a teacher anyway, even if you were one of his favourites. He still had a platform on his right shoe to make up for the defect that left him with legs of uneven length. It meant you could hear him coming along the corridor. Not that it offered any protection.

He told me to sit down. The flimsy plastic chair wobbled. I had expected a communal visiting room, but he had been kept in a separate small room. No wonder, after what he did. The guard stood by the door staring at me like I had done something wrong.

'So, Potty. How are you?'

He was still using that nickname! 'Fine, thank you.'

'And what became of my protégé?'

Is that what he thought of me? I suppose he did pay special attention to me, but there were other boys that he singled out. At least he remembered me. 'I'm a university lecturer now. I had a lot of years in business, but now I teach at university.'

'Well done, Potty!'

'I don't... I mean, I'd prefer it if you'd drop the nickname. It feels odd.'

'What am I to call you?'

'Oh, I, err...'

This wasn't how I'd rehearsed the scene. But then the whole place was not as I expected. No clanging chains and slamming steel doors. No tattooed inmates clanking metal cups against rails in echoing halls. It was more like an old people's home: sparsely furnished, the smell of bleach. The sort of place you visit when you're having CBT or counselling or that new one, mindfulness, where you sit in a chair and listen to your heartbeat. It was that type of municipal building, single-storey, buff brick. Far from the barbed wire and aggressive Scottish guards I had been picturing all this time.

'And which university?'

'Lancaster.'

'Excellent.'

'I always wanted to go there but...'

'But you didn't do well enough in your A-levels. Remind me, what grades did you get?'

'That's not important... I didn't choose...'

'And what are you teaching at Lancaster?'

'Erm... English.'

'Have you written anything of your own?'

'I've published a few short stories.'

'Excellent, Potty. I remember you did have moments in your essays, but lacked the courage to write anything honest.'

'That's not very fair... Anyway, I'm not here to talk about my CV.'

'No, I don't suppose you are. Why are you here? I was intrigued to see the visiting order, and of course I always have time for one of my boys. I have all the time in the world now.' He leaned forward. 'What do you want from me?'

I straightened my tie and looked him straight in the eyes. He stared straight back.

'I want to talk about the truth,' I said.

'Oh dear, still at that stage, are we? Everyone is searching for the truth, dear boy. *Veritas Nunquam Perit.*' He said the school motto with a sigh. 'Truth Never Dies.'

'I want to resolve what happened,' I said. 'Then I can move on.'

'Move on from what?' He always used to add air to the 'wh' in 'w' questions as if he was blowing a kiss. I was supposed to be grilling him, not the other way round.

'You know damn well what!'

'There's no need to raise your voice.'

'I…' For a moment I almost apologised.

'I suppose you've read what they said in the papers,' he said.

I'd reread the story in the Lymm Herald on the train. I felt the folded paper in my blazer pocket. I had almost memorised it.

LYMM TEACHER JAILED FOR SEX ABUSE

A teacher has been jailed for eight years after being convicted for sexually abusing dozens of boys at a Cheshire grammar school.

Reverend Christopher Austin, 62, was found guilty of 22 sex assaults carried out when he was a teacher at St Peter's RC College in Lymm, Cheshire. When the offences took place, between 1973 and 1983, the school was run by Catholic religious order the Brothers of Christ.

The crimes first came to the attention of the Herald in 2010 when one of Austin's victims, a former pupil, contacted police.

Austin, who lived with his mother in Stamford Park View, Altrincham, had denied all charges at Manchester Minshull Street Crown Court.

> Fifty former pupils had presented evidence of corpo-
> ral punishment that led to indecent assaults. Another
> teacher had been cited by victims, but is deceased.
>
> Manchester solicitors Simpson Myers are pursuing
> the school and the local authority for compensation on
> behalf of the victims.

'I notice you did not participate in the court case,' he said.

'That's not what I want...'

'What do you want?'

'I want to try and understand why...'

'Have you been in contact with any of your classmates?'

'No.'

'Not one? I thought it was all social networks and Facebook nowadays. That's how groups of former pupils collude, isn't it?' He rolled his tongue round 'collude' as if to show off his classical education.

'Collude?' I wasn't sure if I'd said it properly. From his expression, it seemed not.

'Do you have a better word?'

'Are you saying they fabricated the case?'

'Are we to conduct a retrial now? Ought we not to leave that to the lawyers?'

'I'm not asking you about the case directly.'

'You don't seem to be asking anything directly at all, dear boy. My little peccadilloes were few and far between, yet dozens of liars and thieves show their faces when there is a crowd to support them.'

I kept trying to say something, but he wouldn't let me speak. I had a recurring nightmare until my thirties of being late for his lesson, running along crowded corridors at school.

'Do you remember Psalms?' he asked.

'Er, no,' I lied.

'They give me solace. You ought to know 109, A Psalm of David.'

I could remember, and he insisted on reciting it.

'"For the mouths of the wicked and the deceitful are opened against me. They have spoken with a lying tongue. They have surrounded me with words of hatred; and fought against me without cause. For my love they act as my accusers; but I give myself unto prayer. Thus they have repaid me evil for good, and hatred for my love."'

'I haven't been a Catholic since I left school,' I told him.

He shook his head. As a reverend, he was bound to take the opposing view. Was he still Reverend? Mum kept up with it till the end, never missed Mass. I stopped going when I finished school and have tried to avoid it since.

'You will always be a Catholic, dear boy.' Then he added a literary quote about the twitch on the thread. At school, twentieth-century literature wasn't a big part of the curriculum, but he had insisted on us reading Waugh.

I changed tack. You can't get anywhere with confrontation. 'You were the only one that ever paid me any attention,' I said.

It was true. He always used to come and stand by my desk, which embarrassed me. Most of the other teachers ignored me. I was only picked out for punishment a handful of times in seven years.

'You seemed like a lost boy to me, so I tried to help you. I tried to help you all.'

Maybe Mum was right. He was her favourite teacher. She always said that discipline was close to Godliness. He was the only one that talked to me alone. But why had so many of those other boys accused him? I mean, yes, he had... done things, but surely not with that many?

'You did go a bit far with the discipline.'

'"You"? Myself alone, or the school collectively?'

'Well, you weren't the only one that used the strap, and there was Mr Castle with his bottom-slayer.'

'It was never more than a gentle reminder. You can't seriously suggest that poor old Sam Castle, God rest his soul, was abusing boys? He patted you on your rumps with a harmless miniature cricket bat as a humorous way of reminding you of certain words.'

'I never did forget DNA.' I almost laughed. He almost smiled. When I had failed to remember it in third-year biology, I had to say 'de-ox-y-ri-bo-nu-cle-ic-a-cid' while Castle hit me ten times. I wasn't allowed to brush the chalk off my trousers all day.

'It's such a shame to bespoil a man's reputation when he is no longer here to defend himself,' he said.

'You don't think he did anything wrong?'

'I'm quite sure he didn't derive any sexual gratification from it, if that's what you're asking. Though I'm positive he was penalised throughout his life for his sexuality. The world was not as liberal then. I'm glad he didn't have to go through this.'

I stared at him. I had my arms folded. He carried on.

'Of course, that's the crux of the case, isn't it? Isn't that why you're here? Are you intending to add your name to the list of claimants?'

'I... no... not at all. I've never told anyone apart from my wife.'

'No, you wouldn't have.'

That irritated me. He had done wrong! Maybe I should have said something sooner, but I felt guilty. That first time I had to go to the headmaster's office, and the gift he gave me.

'I need you to apologise...'

'Apologise? I did everything in my power to help you.' He sighed. 'I tried to help all of you.'

'Do you remember a boy called Simpson?'

'I remember every single one of you. Horrid little urchin, that one. Uncouth. No surprise he became one of those injury solicitors, rousing a rabble for financial gain.'

'I remember one time he approached you at the front of the class to apologise, and you tore him apart.'

Mr Austin looked heavenwards. He almost tutted. He was wearing a grey sweater and blue jeans. I had imagined him in an orange uniform, like in a film. 'Tell me, do you only have bad memories of our time together?'

'Not entirely. I did want to thank you for lending me the books by Poe and Forster.' I was hoping to follow on with literature at university if I had got the grades. No wonder I failed, after what happened. Now I would finally be able to do that.

'I'm glad they were of use to you.'

'It was the only act of kindness any teacher at that place showed me.'

'Interesting how you refer to it as "that place". You still don't seem to appreciate how fortunate you were to be in such an environment.'

'Fortunate? You're in here for eight years – you've been convicted in a court of law.'

'And you have a nice cosy job in a university.' He made a church spire with his fingers. 'Where did you learn how to think? How did you get to university in the first place? It certainly wasn't a God-given right.'

'You can't be suggesting...'

'It's not as though you came from the right background.'

I was suddenly thirsty. It reminded me of how the games teacher, Mr Armstrong, yelled at me for not knowing what position I played in rugby the first week. How could I know? I had never played before. I wasn't one of the prep school bullies. I was never picked for the team. 'Wh... what...?'

He was still attacking me. 'Considering your background, you were fortunate to benefit from the privilege of attending one of the top Catholic grammar schools in the country!'

The increased volume caused the guard to clear his throat. Mr Austin leaned closer and splayed his fingers on the table. There were cigarette burns on the plastic. He almost spat the words through his teeth.

'Most boys of your generation would have been glad to have the education you had. Now a few of your classmates are disappointed with their dull lives in middle age and come back for retribution and financial reward!'

'But… the law… '

'The law is a ass.' Dickens was another of his favourites.

He started again. 'I remember that awful mother of yours. I don't remember ever meeting your father. Whatever happened to them?'

'They've both passed on… in the last couple of years. That's not very kind…'

'I am sorry to hear that, dear boy.'

Mum used to go to parents evenings alone. Dad was away a lot then. She always went on about Mr Austin, how he could be my mentor. 'I'm not sure if you should be saying…'

'Not sure?'

He leaned forward. I sat a bit further back in my chair.

'I remember I had to drive all the way to Warrington one night when you'd missed the last bus after one of my evening soirées. They didn't even have the courtesy to invite me in for a cup of tea.'

I was one of a few selected sixth-formers invited to his house for what he called a 'cheese and wine' gathering along with some former pupils. I set off too late because I'd never drunk wine before. He was complaining about doing the journey once. I had to do it twice a day for seven years because mother insisted I went to the Catholic grammar school. 'They were embarrassed. The house...'

'Your mother lacked even the most basic social graces, swanning around like she belonged in the middle class. She didn't have the first clue.'

'I don't think you should be talking about her like that.'

My first ever knowledge of the school was the day my mother was on the phone interviewing the headmaster before I even started there. The call was cut short. It was the exact moment a boy drowned in the school swimming pool. I'm still afraid of water.

'So you're happy with the way they conditioned you? Timid, devoid of any social skills, unable to properly respect authority, not brave enough to challenge it.'

'I was a child!'

'And you are still angry at your parents now.'

That wasn't fair. I disagreed with the decisions they made about A-level choices, but this was about him. It was his fault.

'How old are you now?' he asked.

'Forty-eight.'

'You are wearing well.' He smiled. There was still a gap between his front teeth.

I started to feel the colour rising in my cheeks. That hadn't happened for years. 'Anyway, it's not about my parents. It's about school.'

'Is it? It seems to me that you are still seeking some kind of acceptance.'

What was he talking about?

'How did you hear about me?' He was still asking me questions.

'What do you mean?'

'If you aren't connected to your classmates, how did you find out about the case?'

'It was in the newspapers and on TV.'

'But you already knew before that?'

'I suppose… I was writing a paper on memory, and I looked up the school.'

'A paper? Remind me again where you learnt to think.'

How could he take that stance? He used to hit us and get off on it. Then there were his private meetings...

He carried on. 'Have you had psychological issues? Perhaps you're hoping that some crude Freudian analysis would allow you to blame someone else for your inadequacies.'

'I don't think…'

'Have you had a family?'

'Yes, I'm married. We weren't blessed with children but we tried to…'

'We didn't turn you gay, then?' he sneered.

'That's not very appropriate…'

'Appropriate? Appropriate! How could you possibly imagine what it has been like to live alone all these years? Then those snivelling little oiks come crawling out of the woodwork…'

He had started to rise from his seat. The guard made a patting gesture with his hand. Mr Austin sat down again and intertwined his fingers. I tried not to look at his hands. He looked straight at me again.

'Why have you come here?'

'I need to know why you…'

'I remember quite clearly. You came to see me a few times for guidance, questions about philosophy. Your mother was concerned, so I took on the responsibility in loco parentis.'

'I did hope that someone might show me…'

'It seems you needed some attention, exactly like the others.'

'What do you mean?' Now the guard raised his eyebrows at me.

'I… I was afraid of you, and you… you took advantage!' There, I'd said it. I can still see Our Lady's toes in front of my face as he…

'Boo-hoo. Why don't you grow up?' He scoffed. 'You're as pathetic as the rest of them. I always thought you could have been special. Instead you found excuses not to apply yourself and settled for mediocrity.'

'That's not true. I might have fitted in better if you hadn't…'

'If what?' He shook his head. 'You are such a disappointment to me.' He stood up and lifted his head at the guard.

That wasn't what was supposed to happen. I wanted him to say something. I'll discuss this at counselling on Thursday. She'll probably tell me to sit quietly and breathe. Whenever I do that, I start to panic. Maybe I will write about this instead.

Mr Austin turned his back on me.

I stood for a moment alone.

Then the guard let me out of the room and locked the door noisily behind me.

13.0 Matching Criteria and Final Recommendation

Please complete the Matching Criteria and Special Needs Matching Considerations forms 15.2 and 15.3 (formerly forms B3 and C2) on pages 46 and 48 of the Prospective Adopter's Report (PAR).

These forms allow you to consider your own preferences in terms of age, gender and ethnicity of a child. There is also a list of some of the common special needs of adopted children. You should take time to look these up on the Internet, so you can make informed decisions about whether you feel you would be able to provide for a child with certain special emotional, physical or psychological needs. You must be completely honest and indicate whether for each you 'Would Accept', 'Would Not Accept' or 'Would Consider'. You must not tick that you would accept a child with a particular set of special needs unless you are absolutely certain that you are comfortable with that decision and that you are equipped to provide the best possible environment for a child with those needs. Your allocated social worker will help you to understand these forms.

It will not be held against you if you state that you are unable to consider children with certain categories – remember, honesty is always best – but it may limit the number of potential matches, and you need to think carefully about your reasons. It is important to remember that many children in care have suffered some neglect or abuse or have physical or emotional impairment, so you need to be realistic in your criteria and in your expectations.

Once these tables are complete your social worker will add their own comments and the references and then return the whole Prospective Adopter's Report for you to sign. In accordance with the Statutory Guidelines you will be given seven days in which to comment on the report. After that the social worker will arrange a panel slot, which is normally within two months, depending on availability of the allocated social worker and panel members. After the panel interview, the panel will make a formal recommendation. Subject to the recommendation of the panel chair, the final decision will be formalised by the Agency Decision Maker and communicated to you within one week.

The appeals process is clearly explained on the Council's website.

Special Needs Matching Considerations *To be completed by prospective adopters following discussion with allocated Social Worker. See Fostering and Adoption Guidance Notes pages 43–46*	Would accept	Would not accept	Would consider
Child's Medical History / Medical Records			
Multiple Sclerosis			
Cerebral Palsy			
Severe/chronic/complex medical condition			
HIV / AIDS			
Hepatitis B			
Hepatitis C			
Mobility Impairment			
Severe physical disability			
Minor physical disability			
Downs Syndrome			
Deafness or partial hearing impairment			
Blindness or partial sight impairment			
Hereditary / Parental / Family History			
Severe learning difficulties in parents			
Foetal Alcohol Syndrome (known or suspected)			
Parental drug or alcohol misuse history			
Parental schizophrenia			
Microcephaly (MCPH)			
Learning / Functioning			
ADHD and other behavioural disorders			
Special Educational Needs			
Severe or profound learning disability			
Mild or moderate learning disability			
Autistic Spectrum Disorder / Asperger Syndrome			
Child's History / Past Experience			
Attachment issues			
Physical Abuse			
Sexual Abuse			

Sealed With a Kiss

It is Sunday evening in David and Cici's house. The downstairs is open-plan, painted white with a vermilion accent wall. A family area, with engineered oak flooring and housing two cream leather sofas, runs through into a dining area and a vast modern kitchen. There are three framed photos of Cici in traditional Chinese wedding clothes above the sofas. The kitchen cupboard doors have coffee-coloured lacquer finish. The worktops are white marble. An extractor fan is whirring above a range-style cooker. Its hood shows the stains of frequent use. Glass cooking bowls and chopping boards are spread over a central island. They are making dinner.

Cici scrapes finely diced onions with a cleaver into a wok on the largest of the five burners on the hob, causing a loud hiss. David lifts her long hair, kisses her neck, slips a red apron with a Chinese dragon motif over her head and wraps the tie twice round her waist.

'This whole process is a bloody nightmare,' he says. 'First I have to build a fence 'cause of the pond, now all this past relationship stuff.'

'We're nearly there now.' Cici throws three dried chillies onto the onions and sprinkles some spices. 'We will get a baby soon.'

He says, 'It'll be another year, at this rate. I know they had to contact Alice because I raised Danny, but this latest nonsense is too much.' He leans over from her left; she leans right, in sync. He throws diced garlic and more chopped fresh red chillies into the wok.

She adds a cubed yellow pepper from a small plate. 'I'm not happy about them contacting Gordon either.'

He takes the plate from her. 'I don't want them asking Pippa whether she thinks I'm suitable to adopt a child. What do they expect her to say after twenty years?'

'You don't have a thing to hide, do you?' she says.

He holds out a bowl full of prawns that have been marinating in a brown sauce. She takes it without looking and adds the prawns and a gush of light soy sauce straight from the bottle.

'It's all right for you. You're friendly with Gordon the moron, your Facebook friend,' David says. He quickly washes the plate and bowl and thoroughly scrubs a thick oak chopping board in very hot water.

'I prefer not to fall out with someone. That's all,' she says. 'You know I had only come here recently from China when I met him.' She scrapes the prawn stir-fry into a serving dish with a wooden spoon. 'And he's not…'

He breaks three eggs into a deep bowl and begins to whisk. 'Is that why you kept going all the way to Leeds to see him?'

She gently takes the whisk off him and mixes the eggs at several times his speed. He washes the wok and wipes it inside and out with kitchen roll.

'I told you about it. I don't have a secret.' She pours olive oil into the wok the second he puts it back on the hob.

'Neither do I.'

'Are you sure? Did you tell me every one girl?'

He doesn't make eye contact as he brushes a plate of freshly chopped tomatoes and thinly cut spring onions into the eggs. 'None of them were like you.' He kisses her cheek.

'No one would put up with you being grumpy, more like it.'

A rice cooker clicks, and a red 'cook' light is replaced with an amber 'warm' one.

'I've a good mind to tell the council to forget it,' he says.

'It's nearly the end. We can finish it,' Cici says.

He takes two patterned blue bowls from a high-level cupboard and two pairs of chopsticks from a drawer. She serves the egg-to-mato dish and clicks off the fan.

He unties the apron and washes the wok again.

* * *

The social worker opens her lined notepad on the dining table and creases back the page. Frayed cuffs of her white blouse peep out from her M&S suit jacket. Cici and David are sitting next to other each. She is wearing a fitted black suit. He has on a blue cotton Oxford shirt. There are various papers strewn across the table. This is their fourth meeting. On the wall behind the social worker is a multi-aperture photo frame that holds pictures of Cici and David in various family clusters, one of Cici buried under a group of four blue-eyed children.

'So, I'm afraid there's still a problem with the pond,' the social worker says.

'But I've built a fence with a lockable gate. It ruins the garden,' David says.

'The issue is that an older child could climb over the wall further along.' She uses the tone of a primary school teacher. 'It only takes a second to drown.'

'If they were determined to kill themselves... But then they could run down to the river and throw themselves in.'

'We can't do anything about the river though, can we?'

Cici joins in. 'Tracey, we want to adopt a baby. How can they get over that wall?'

'Babies soon become toddlers. You'd be surprised what they can get up to.'

David sighs. 'What have I got to do now?'

'So, Health and Safety are going to send someone down to do

an inspection. Also, I've asked Legal if they can draw up a document for you to sign that indemnifies the Council.'

David stares at the table. He wants to say that indemnifying the council is really not the point, but Cici has made him promise not to argue.

'So, moving on, let's look at your relationship chronologies.'

Tracey turns back several pages of her pad. Cici's eyes remind David to be calm.

'So, I've talked to Alice, and I'm satisfied that everything is fine there. It will act in your favour that you've stayed in touch with Danny all these years, and I can tell you're fond of him.'

'Did she admit to her drinking?' David asks.

'We had a long and open conversation. Obviously I can't repeat what she said.'

'Can I see the reference?'

'That's confidential. So, can we move on and look at your other relationships?'

Cici says, 'I emailed you Gordon's details, and I texted him.' She glances at David.

'Yes, I've got that, thank you,' Tracey says. 'I'll write to him. So, David, we've dealt with Alice. What about your first wife?' She smiles, pen poised.

'Tracey, I'm struggling with the whole concept. Pippa was over twenty years ago. I've no idea where she lives now or even what name she goes by.'

'As long as we can fill in what her last known address was.'

'That'll be our house in 1995.' He taps a long list of addresses on a form. 'That one, Brooks Drive. I don't know where she's lived since.'

'I see. By the way, did you manage to find out the postcode for the flat you had before that one?'

'I really can't remember. I was only there six months.'

'Haven't you kept any record?'

He closes his eyes for a few seconds before replying. 'Do you keep your utility bills for twenty-five years?'

She raises her eyebrows and scratches a cross on her form. 'You said Pippa's parents lived in the biggest house in their village in Suffolk?'

David takes a deep breath. 'I've no idea if they still live there. Her dad'll probably be dead, he had liver problems.'

'Still, if we can at least try?' Tracey makes another note.

David sits forward, fingers spread on his thighs. 'All these years have gone by and now I have to write to them...'

'You don't have to do anything. We'll send the letter.'

'What will you say? "Dear Henry and Bunny, remember that northern lad that married your daughter twenty-five years ago, and she left him for another man?"' He makes no attempt to hide the contempt in his voice. '"We'd like to get in touch with her to see if she feels it's appropriate for him to adopt a child."'

'It isn't like that at all, David. The new head of department insists we do this for all cases. There was a case at her previous authority. We need to contact all previous significant relationships.'

'She had an affair and left me. Now she gets to know all about my life.'

'We won't give away any confidential information.'

'Only that I live in Lancashire, I'm adopting a child, I'm married, my wife's full name, so she can look up Cici on Facebook and LinkedIn, and find out my career history, contact my sisters, know which friends I kept in touch with, see pictures of our holidays...'

'I can't change the process. Besides, she's probably moved on. Like you say, it was a long time ago.'

* * *

David and Dougie are wearing suits with narrow lapels and are smoking in a wine bar. Robson and Jerome are singing Unchained Melody on a small TV in the background.

'What did Pippa say when you confronted her, Columbo?' *Dougie's Geordie accent is pronounced.*

'She laughed.'

'Bitch!'

'She said it was a nervous laugh. She'd obviously had a drink.'

'I bet she had. Least you haven't got kids.'

'That's off the agenda for a few years.' *David takes a gulp of Stella from an ornate glass.*

Dougie settles back in his chair. 'What's the other fella's wife like?'

'Wendy? She's nice, redhead. Few years older...'

'Well, you know what I think?'

'Go on.'

'Least you can do is go round and scuttle his wife.'

They laugh.

'That should get it out of your system.' *Dougie raises his glass.*

'I don't know if she even knows about it yet.'

'Doesn't she have a right to know?'

'I suppose I ought to go round and console her. They've got a daughter too.'

'You're a gentleman. Besides, what's the worst that can happen?'

'He's hardly going to come round and beat me up.'

'Exactly! What can he say?'

'I believe you're sleeping with my wife...'

'You started it!'

Another round of laughter.

'How old's the daughter?'

'Fifteen, I think. She's had some problems.'

'Well, if the wife doesn't give you satisfaction...'

'*Dougie, do you remember that chat we had about The Line?*'

'*The line?*' He scratches his head. '*Vaguely. You know what I always say.*'

'*I'm going to regret this.*'

'*If there's grass on the pitch...*'

* * *

'You need to calm down. I don't want Tracey to see your bad temper.' Cici is applying her make-up. Chris Evans is cheerfully chatting with a child on the radio. David is under a white duvet with a cherry-tree design. On the wall above him is a framed cartoon pencil portrait of Cici in a beret with the Eiffel Tower sketched behind her.

'Why do they have to go raking over our exes?' he says. 'What if Pippa says something about that car accident?'

'I think it is best to tell Tracey.' She buttons her work shirt.

'It didn't show up on the DBS check, and the woman dropped the claim.' His eyes are on the last few leaves of the sycamore outside the bedroom window. It has taken all year. They have still not completed the application process.

Cici is answering a text, smiling.

David frowns. 'Who are you texting?'

'Nobody.'

'I bet you haven't told Tracey all your secrets.'

'I did.'

'Even about what you got up to when you first met Gordon?'

'I only just arrived in UK.'

'*The* UK...'

She turns and gives him a stare.

'You said not to stop correcting you.'

'When's the Health and Safety man coming about the fence?'

149

'Thursday. They expect me to be in all day.'

'Try to be nice. You only make things worse.'

* * *

'So, David, this is our last one-to-one session.' Tracey clicks her pen. 'We've covered finance and we've got both of your work references. I've made a note that we need to see your tax return when it's completed. I don't think there is anything to add about education?'

David straightens a coaster on the table. 'No.'

'So, can we look again at your past relationships?' She sounds like a kids' TV presenter reading a story. 'You say that Pippa left you for another man? Why was that?'

'You'd have to ask her.'

'I'm sure you'll agree there are always two sides.'

'She was sleeping with someone else. How's that two-sided?'

'I have to produce a balanced report.'

'Is it absolutely necessary to contact her?'

'It's the procedure. So, moving on, who's Wendy? You've listed her after Pippa.' Tracey takes a sip of tea.

'Tracey, that was a short-term thing, a rebound.'

'So, why did you include her?'

'You said to write the chronologies with no gaps, I didn't expect you to contact them all.'

'I didn't either,' she sighs. 'Why don't you tell me about her, and I can decide if we need to include it.'

David shakes his head, eyes closed. Arguments and shouting come back to him. 'She was the wife of the man... Pippa's boss, Vince, the one she ran off with. They ruined Wendy's life, left her alone with a daughter...'

'So, what happened between you two?'

David takes a deep breath. 'Wendy was angry. She hadn't got over her husband…'

Tracey is filling line after line of her A4 pad. 'We do understand that exes might not always say the nicest things. So, did you leave her then?'

'I had to… It was complicated. She couldn't have more kids, and there was her daughter.' He doesn't make eye contact.

'Did you spend a lot of time with her daughter?'

'Leah? No, not a lot. She had some disciplinary problems at school.' He stops and looks into space for a moment. 'She would have been all grown up now.'

'Would have been?

'She died.'

'While you and her mum were together?'

'No…' He stops himself. 'It was in the local paper a few years later. Overdose. She was only nineteen.'

He looks at Tracey while she writes, but his mind has drifted away.

* * *

David is wearing a grey suit and reading a typed report. His hair is dark brown. On the wall behind him is a map of the UK with stickers in various colours. Papers and folders cover half of his wide desk. A huge computer monitor is turned off. A Motorola phone is connected to a bulky charger next to the monitor. A desk phone rings. He answers with a formal 'Hello.'

'Hi, David, it's Wendy. I hope you don't mind me calling you at work?'

'Of course not. I haven't seen you since Vince's barbeque.' He stands up and shuts his office door, automatically straightening his green and blue striped tie.

'I'm afraid I got a bit squiffy that night!'

'Hey, you were having fun. Leah's growing up.'

'I worry about that girl. She's growing up too fast. She was caught smoking at school. I worry it's not just cigarettes. Listen, David, I need to talk to you about something more serious.'

'Ah.' He sits back down and leans back.

'I think Vince might be having an affair with Pippa.'

'I was wondering whether to call you.' He taps his pen on the desk and looks at a handwritten to do list. There are circles around the word Wendy. 'How long have you suspected?'

'I've wondered for a while. Did you know?'

'I saw their cars parked together the other night outside the Griffin and confronted her when she got in. I wasn't sure if I should tell you, you know, with Leah and everything.'

'It's going to kill her; she worships her dad. Listen, David, can we meet face to face? I'm at work, I can't really talk.'

'Of course, it would be nice to see you again.' He smiles for the first time in weeks. 'Are you free at lunchtime?'

'Can we make it tomorrow? I'm a bit scruffy today. We're doing stock-taking.'

'Tomorrow, 12.30, the Yew Tree?'

'I'll look forward to it.'

* * *

Cici shakes her umbrella and slips into the passenger seat. She leans over and they kiss. David starts talking before they have left the station car park.

'I'm not happy with you speaking to Gordon. I want you to promise you won't go and see him.'

David's statement has been simmering all afternoon. Cici hasn't even fastened her seatbelt.

'Don't be jealous.'

'I've got good reason, haven't I?'

'He'll give a good reference if I'm nice to him.'

'We all know what that means.'

'He will help. He was adopted himself.'

'Look how he turned out.'

'What about your many exes? You never even said about Wendy. I didn't know she was a significant relationship.'

'I should never have mentioned her... Hey!' He beeps his horn. 'Don't mind me, I'll brake sharply! Bloody taxis.' He turns to Cici. 'Do you need anything from the shop?'

'Didn't you go to Sainsbury's?'

'How could I? I had to wait all day for the Health and Safety man. He finally turned up at four.'

'What did he say?'

'I'm going to have to put another fence and a lockable gate in front of the house.'

She gazes through the window into the darkness.

He turns the radio up.

'Hey, this is an oldie... Bryan Hyland, *Sealed With a Kiss.*' He sings along absent-mindedly.

'What happened with Wendy?'

'She couldn't have any more kids – she'd had that operation.'

'That operation? You mean hysterectomy? Thanks for your sympathy.'

'You know I don't mean it like that.' Their eyes meet. 'At least that's all over with now.'

She touches his hand. 'I hope so. What about her daughter?'

'She would have been nearly your age. She was a teenager then.

'What do you mean, "would have been"?'

'Hm? There was a story in the Evening News a few years later.' He stares straight ahead. 'She died of an overdose.'

Cici watches the naked trees hurry past the window in the darkness.

David starts singing again.

'You're putting all your heart into that,' Cici says. 'Who are you thinking about?'

'Thinking about the good old days.'

'"Old" is the operating word.'

David's mind floats back to another time, another version of the song.

Cici turns the radio down. 'Do you agree about a girl now?'

'Where did that come from?'

'You had practice with your ex.'

'It's thirty here, idiot, not sixty!' He makes a gesture through the window. 'I spent much more time with Danny. I still think we should say we'll accept either.'

'I prefer a girl.'

'If that's what you want. Girls love their daddies best anyway.'

'And I want to see a picture before we decide.'

'Of course.'

Sealed With a Kiss comes to an end and Cici kisses her fingers and presses them onto his cheek.

He rubs it off and sticks his tongue out. He doesn't speak again for the rest of the journey home.

* * *

Tracey puts the lid on her black Bic biro and puts it down on top of her pad. Rain is battering the window. Outside a new timber fence blocks half of the view.

'So, is there anything else you want to discuss, either of you?'

David thinks about the peony he planted on Cici's birthday five years ago. It produces one giant flower every April, but she can't see it anymore because of the fence. Cici nudges his arm.

'There is something.' He looks down at the table.

Tracey says, 'I'm sure we'll be able to deal with it, so long as you're completely open.'

David says, 'If you contact Pippa, she might mention something that happened at the end.'

'I'm listening.'

'There was an accident...' He sighs.

'It's all right.'

'It was a difficult time.' He reaches for his tea.

'I understand.'

David tells about how he and Pippa were being civilised. She was about to move out. They had gone out to eat. They had a car accident. It was a known accident spot. It was the other driver's fault. Both cars were write-offs.

Tracey listens patiently. 'That must have been scary.'

'Exactly – scary, that's it. I was in shock.'

'Was anyone hurt?'

'No one was hurt in the accident. I got a sore knee. It all got a bit heated. The woman and Pippa were shouting at each other. There was a bit of pushing and shoving...'

'Go on.'

'I was trying to calm everything down, and I pushed the woman away... to stop them fighting, and she sort of... fell and banged her head.'

'Oh dear!'

'She was knocked out for a minute. Afterwards she got all unreasonable, said I hurt her deliberately, got the police and solicitors involved.'

'I see.' Tracey reaches for her pen.

'No, no, it wasn't that bad. They dropped the case. There was no evidence, and Pippa told them she hadn't seen anything. It was an accident.'

'I'll have to speak to my supervisor.' Tracey smiles. 'Hopefully it won't delay panel.'

* * *

A new silver BMW is squealing as it reverses down the drive of a large mock-Tudor house at speed.

'That's right, run away, you fucking bloody coward!' Wendy flings a man's suit jacket after the car as it scurries down the drive, engine wailing.

'Don't you ever come near me or my daughter ever again! Bastard!' She kicks wildly at the front of the car but misses and falls over, sobbing.

'If I ever see you near this house again, I'll call the police…!' She is back on her feet, stumbling towards the road. The car's brake lights throw a red glow over her for a moment.

'After what you've done to me, I hope you go to hell with that bitch!'

The car slides away into the night.

'I'll never forgive you… You hear me… never!'

A teenage girl's face peers round the front door. Eye make-up is smeared all over her cheeks.

'Get inside, Leah!' Wendy yells.

* * *

Cici is reading out items from a printed list, pen poised over her dinner plate. Her food has barely been touched.

'I don't think I could cope with a deaf child,' she says.

'Sometimes kids have those grommets and they grow out of it. Danny had them.'

'All right, I'll tick 'Would consider'. Next, physical disability?'

'Again, depends how severe.' There is uneaten food on David's plate too. He is poking at it with his fork, separating green beans from the rest of the meal.

'I think we should say no,' Cici says.

'It might be minor... you know, like, one limb.'

'I don't want a child with one arm!'

'No, I mean, maybe a club-foot or something that they can treat.'

'You would be happy to have a girl with a bad leg?'

'Or boy.'

'Girl.'

'All right... girl.'

'I'm okay with emotional things. I worry about a handicapped child,' she says. 'I don't know what to do.' She strokes the back of her left hand with her right.

'At least a disabled child wouldn't be able to climb over the elaborate system of fences and gates I've had to erect.'

Cici sighs. 'Let it go about the fence.'

David looks through the kitchen window at the garden. He thinks of long days of digging to plant shrubs and trees. The winter-flowering plum tree he planted because Cici likes the magenta blossom is now completely obscured by the new gate.

'We're nearly there. We can do it.' She puts her hand on his fist.

He unclenches his hand. 'Carry on.'

'Severe learning difficulties?

'What, like Gordon, you mean?

She asks again, without looking up. 'You okay with a child that can't read and write?'

David sighs loudly. 'They don't have to be top of the class. As long as I can read her bedtime stories.'

'What about when she's grown up? Can we look after a grown

up with learning problems when you get old?'

And so they continue. The dinner plates are ignored. They debate the degrees of emotional difficulties they could cope with and agree to tick 'Would accept' for experience of neglect and emotional difficulties, on the basis that they might apply to every child. They look up foetal alcohol syndrome on Cici's tablet and tick the right-hand column again. Severe emotional difficulties is also marked 'Would consider'.

'Last one: sexualised behaviour. What does it mean?'

David fidgets in his chair. 'Like if a teenage girl has seen bad behaviour and acts like that with men for attention...'

'How do you know?'

David fiddles with his pen. 'There was something on the second course about it: one of those fostering case studies, remember?' He stands up and picks up their plates. 'Probably wouldn't come up with the ages we're looking for. Come on, let's get this finished.'

'I'll tick 'Would accept'. Okay, done! We already did the ethnicity and religion page.'

'Are you still okay with mixed race?' he asks.

'Why not? We don't look like each other anyway,' she says.

He pulls a funny face.

Cici signs the form and passes it to David. He turns the pages, skim-reading.

'They won't ever ask about... you know... about school?'

He tries to stop images of the headmaster's office from entering his mind. He can see the toes of Our Lady's statue above him. One of the toes is chipped.

Cici stands and puts her arms around him. 'Don't worry. Nobody ever knows about that.' She strokes his hair like you would a pet dog. 'You already did your education part with Tracey. She's not even allowed to ask about your counselling.'

He closes his eyes while she comforts him.

'That's all in the very far past,' she says.

* * *

Tracey's palms are together as if in prayer. There are three mugs of tea on the table.

'So, the good news is, I've checked about the accident in 1995, and as no charges were brought, it doesn't affect your DBS check.'

David sighs loudly. 'Thanks for being so understanding, Tracey.'

'We do accept that people are human, you know.'

Cici glances at David across the papers on the table. 'Is there anything else we have to do?'

'So, the chronologies are finished. We've got a reference from Gordon.'

The two women share a smile.

'We've had no reply from Pippa's family after three weeks. That's all we can do without a full search, and I don't want to delay Stage 2 any longer.' She ticks an item on her list. 'I've taken Wendy off the list since you didn't live together, and it was only six months.'

David breathes out.

'Are we finished with Stage 2 then?' Cici is almost out of her chair.

'Yes, I just need a copy of your new gas safety certificate.'

Cici hands over a pink form. David picks up an invoice. He thinks of Cici's phrase about money burning your pocket.

'What about the fire safety question?' David's voice is assertive. 'When the fire brigade came they said we shouldn't have a fire-extinguisher, it was safer to let them deal with it, but the form requires that we have one, so I'd already bought one.'

Tracey's eyes look to her right. 'So, I think the best answer is to keep it but don't use it, and I'll bring that up at the next team meeting. I have your fire escape plan.'

David wants to tell her that a twelve-month-old baby can't read a fire escape plan and that this is the second time they have paid £100 for a gas safety certificate.

'Also, Cici, we agreed you would add business insurance to your car insurance to cover you in case we go the fostering-for-adoption route.'

'Do I need it even before we are approved?' Cici asks.

'I think it would be better, don't you?'

'All right, I'll do that.' She ignores David's head movement. 'What happens now?'

'So, you both have a chance to comment on the report. I'll email it you next week. I'll try and make sure you have a full week, but I don't work Thursdays, and there's a back-log in admin, so it might be a day late. I'll submit the report, and we're all set for the next panel date. I'm afraid the panel for December is full, so it will probably be January.'

'That's great news.' David grabs Cici's hand. 'It's been hard work.'

'Of course, there are no guarantees, but I'm sure it will be worth it in the end,' Tracey says. 'And you've decided your preference is for a girl?'

They look at each other and nod in unison.

* * *

It is early evening in the mock-Tudor house. The front room door opens.

'David? Can you help me with something?' Her voice is baby-ish. The girl closes the door and leans against it with her hands behind her back. She is wearing too much mascara.

'Hi, Leah. What's up?'

Jason Donovan is straining his voice on the television.

'Ooh, I love this one!' She starts to sing along to *Sealed With a Kiss.*

'I don't suppose you've heard the original sixties version?' David says.

'This one is miles better!'

'If you say so.' He grins.

'David? Can you give me some advice?'

'Of course I can, sweetheart. What is it?'

'It's about me and Matty.' She sways while she speaks.

'Have you talked to your mum?'

'No way! You've got to promise you won't tell her when she gets back from work.'

'All right. My lips are sealed. What's up?'

'It's about… you know.'

'What?

'Erm… sex.'

She curls up next to him on the sofa, tucking her legs under herself. Her knees are exposed between her grey skirt and short white socks. David clears his throat and sits more upright.

'Can't you talk to your mum about contraception?' he says.

'It's not that. She knows we're going to. She even said I can go on the pill. She says I'm allowed now I'm sixteen.'

He turns to face her. 'What is it then?'

'I want the first time to be special. I want to wait till the end-of-year disco, but Matty's getting frustrated. I'm frightened he'll do it with someone else.'

'I'm sure he won't. You can tell he dotes on you. Besides, you're the prettiest of all of your friends.'

She blushes and touches his hand. 'Thank you, David.'

'Doesn't he, you know… Boys have a way… I mean, all boys do it…'

'That's the thing… he says he wants me to.'

'He wants you to…?'

'He wants me to touch him.' She looks down at his crotch.

He crosses his legs and clears his throat. 'How do you feel about that?'

'It's…'

'It's all right, you can tell me.'

Leah crosses her slender arms. 'I know I should give in, but I don't know what to do.'

'Is that all you're worried about?' He laughs.

'It's not funny!'

'I'm sorry, sweetheart.' He squeezes her arm.

'I might do it wrong.'

'I'm sure you won't. Ask him to show you.'

'David?' She presses her naked calf against him. 'Can I… will you… teach me?'

He looks at the door. 'Leah, I'm really not sure if…'

'I won't tell anyone, ever, I promise. Cross my heart.'

She draws a line from breast to breast and another vertically down her cleavage. His eyes follow. She is wearing freshly applied blood-red nail varnish.

'I think we should stop this conversation before it gets out of hand.'

'Don't you like me?'

'Leah, it's not that, you're a sexy girl, any man would love to… but we shouldn't even be talking like this.'

'Wouldn't you like it?'

David looks at the door again then at the drawn curtains. 'Leah, that's not the question…'

'Nobody wants to help me!'

'Don't be like that. You know I'll do everything in my power to help you.'

'Why don't you then?

'Look… if we… it might lead to…'

She puts her hand on his thigh. He firmly takes it off again.

'Can I...'

She undoes the second button of her white school blouse exposing a black bra.

'Leah, no...'

Her hand in his hair disconnects his speech function momentarily.

'Jesus, Leah. If anyone ever found out we even had this conversation...'

'I know!' Her hand is spidering up his leg.

'Leah, stop, we mustn't.'

He stands up, glancing down to check that his physical reaction isn't too obvious.

'You'd better go to bed.'

'Nobody loves me!' She stands up next to him. He towers over her.

'It's not that. You must understand.'

Tears start to wet her face. He takes her narrow shoulders in his hands.

'Talk to Matty. Everything will be all right.'

'I will,' she sniffs. 'You won't tell Mummy, will you?' She nestles into his chest.

'Of course not. And you must never tell a soul,' he whispers. 'On pain of death.'

'Cross my heart and hope to die.'

She makes another cross, the downward stroke of her finger causing her blouse to open further.

'Promise?'

'Promise,' she pouts. 'Sealed with a kiss...'

* * *

'I can't believe what's she's put!' David slaps the thick document in his hand. He is standing in the kitchen.

'It's completely different to what you said.' Cici puts down her work bag and a Waitrose carrier bag full of groceries.

David puts the report on the centre island and picks up the shopping. 'Can you believe that stuff about my behaviour causing Alice's drinking?' David says. He begins to unpack vegetables.

'I know! They must know about her drink-driving before she met you.'

'How hard can it be to check police records?'

'Did you see all this she says about Gordon?' She turns the pages of the report. 'Here… "Gordon says he felt neglected because of Cici's ambition." He was the one who went to prostitutes!'

They are both walking around the centre island. David is opening cupboards and putting the shopping away. Cici still has her coat on. David snatches up the report from the island.

'Listen to this: "Vulnerabilities… David has been divorced twice and was ill-equipped to deal with his responsibilities. He now accepts full responsibility for his own failings!" What the fuck?'

'What does this mean?' Cici points at a paragraph. '"Potential communication difficulties owing to language"?'

'She's probably being racist. Do we have difficulties?'

'Only about "the". Did you call adoption helpline?' Cici asks.

'The adoption helpline.'

'Not now!'

'They said as long as the report has a favourable recommendation, we should sign it.'

'I don't think it's right. And she's says either sex… and age up to four! That's not what we agreed.'

'The problem is, prospective adopters have no rights until panel – that helpline woman said so. If we don't sign it, we can't even make a complaint.'

'I don't want to sign it,' she says. 'How long have we got to reply?'

'It's supposed to be a week but she has to send it off on Wednesday.'

'I will fill in some comments.'

'Let's do that,' David says. He folds the empty carrier bags and puts them in a drawer.

She puts the report on the table and takes her coat off. 'Did you book Heathcotes?'

'No, they won't be full on a Monday.'

Cici looks at the floor. 'Doesn't feel like happy anniversary. Thanks for the flowers, by the way. The girls all said nice things about you.'

'Shall we leave the meal then?'

'Let's wait till this is all over.'

'We said that last year.' He puts his arms round her.

A tear dribbles down her cheek. He gently wipes it away with his little finger.

* * *

The boardroom in County Hall is a grand Victorian space with an enormous polished wood table in the centre and worn oak panelling. The chairwoman has a generous smile.

'Good morning, and welcome!'

Cici and David shuffle to their seats and mumble 'Good morning' together.

'Relax. This is a very informal panel,' the chairwoman says. All around the table are eight casually dressed women, most of them wearing scarves, all overdoing their smiles. David and Cici intertwine their fingers under the table. He wants to make a joke about equal opportunities, but remembers he's in character and stops himself.

The chairwoman continues. 'This meeting is a friendly chat to make sure everybody is comfortable going forward. We'll ask you a few questions and then we'll see if we can move forward. Is that all right?'

David looks at Cici and says, 'Yes, thank you. That's very clear.' Cici nods.

'I see that you've stayed in touch with your stepson, Danny. That's very positive. I can see from his mother's reference that there are no issues there.'

David forces a smile.

'It seems you had a bit of fun with a fence?'

David tenses and turns to Cici. She squeezes his hand and speaks up. 'David did lots of work to make the garden safe. I think it was very unnecessary to build two gates.'

David says, 'At least it's safe now.'

'I'm glad to see that you have been flexible,' the chairwoman says. 'Now, I'll introduce the members of the panel. Then we'll go round the table. I notice there are no comments from you on the report, so it should be straightforward.'

Cici's eyes widen at the words 'no comments'. She stares at David, who shrugs and keeps his lips tightly together.

David stares at the high cold ceiling, ornate cornice details and an elaborate ceiling rose, the original sash windows painted over several times. Rain patters insistently against the windows while Cici and David give predictable answers to a series of bland questions. David doesn't look at Tracey once. 'Just be yourself,' she had said on the way along the corridor. There is a circular clock above the chairwoman. David holds his breath each time the second hand stutters past the twelve. Cici holds his hand under the table throughout.

One of the women, who had been introduced with a lengthy title including the word 'education', speaks up. 'I have one question.

David, I see that you have begun a university career, which is to be commended. In one of your meetings with Tracey you mentioned you had "troubled" times at school and that you "hated" your experience at St Peter's. Given that you are now working in education, I just wanted to clarify that.'

David looks at Cici. He opens his mouth, but no noise comes out. His eyes focus on a knot in the table. He can smell furniture polish.

Tracey clears her throat and rummages with her notebook. 'We did speak about that briefly, didn't we?'

'Do we have to drag that up now?' David's face is reddening. He pulls his hand away from Cici.

Cici frowns. 'It's all right.' She holds his arm. 'It's all right, David, I know.'

The chairwoman becomes serious. 'Tracey?'

Tracey is frantically turning pages of her notebook. 'I'm trying to find my notes.'

Two of the ladies in scarves mutter to each other. David is breathing heavily. His leg is shaking. Cici is struggling to keep him still.

Tracey says, 'David spoke about some issues at school. He mentioned that one of his teachers had recently been on trial... He didn't disclose... I didn't think...'

He blurts, 'I thought it was supposed to be confidential!'

Tracey is wide-eyed. 'I don't know what...'

'I didn't want to have to talk about that ever again!' David starts to get up from his seat. Cici tries to restrain him.

He splutters, 'It was thirty-five years ago!' He grabs his coat and scarf.

Cici tries to catch him as he strides towards the door. 'Wait, David!'

'I especially didn't want to have to talk about that to an entire audience!' He turns and faces the room before Cici can catch him. 'What happened to privacy?' He pauses. Twenty eyes are looking at him.

He yells, 'I was abused at school!' He spits his last words at Tracey, 'There! Is that what you want? Are you happy now?'

Two minutes later Cici and David are spat out into the rain outside County Hall. They walk, unspeaking, huddled beneath an umbrella under the shadow of the stone building. She is clutching his arm in hers.

A lady in a raincoat hurries past in the opposite direction holding a little brown dog close to her bosom. She smiles at Cici.

David and Cici's eyes meet.

* * *

Barbara Townsend
Adoption Agency Decision Maker
███████████ Council
Directorate for Children & Young Adults
PO Box ███████████████

CONFIDENTIAL

Mr DJ Potter & Ms C Shen

███████████████
███████████████
██████████
███████████
█████████

13 April 2015

Dear David and Cici

I refer to your adoption panel on 24 February. Following the panel meeting there are a number of matters that I feel must be resolved before I am able to recommend your approval to the Board.

Primary amongst these is a feeling that David has not properly faced his own past in relation to apparent personal matters going back to his time at school. Members of the panel were concerned to see David's outburst during the panel meeting, and it is evident that further investigations must take place before it is possible to proceed towards approval.

I am gravely concerned that a matter of this importance has been kept secret from your social worker, which indicates a breakdown in trust. The Council cannot approve any individual unless we have confidence in your relationship with the social worker.

It is my recommendation that your allocated social worker, Tracey Wapshot, arrange an urgent meeting with you both, during office hours in the next month, to discuss a plan going forward, including a series of further meetings with you individually and together. She may recommend further counselling for David given that he has clearly not fully dealt with certain issues from his own past. This does not mean that you may not eventually be approved, and I am sympathetic about what must be a difficult situation. However, it is my duty to ensure that there is no risk of any instability in an adoptive family.

Unfortunately, these additional steps mean that a number of statutory checks will have expired by the time the process is completed, as it is now almost two years since your initial registration. I understand that the process has taken longer in your case than the average period because of difficulties finding dates for training courses, the Council's reorganisation, and the new ICT strategy, which are beyond our control.

DBS checks will need to be repeated for each of you, as will financial records and medical reports, especially as Cici has had ongoing medical issues. It is the responsibility of the prospective adopter to pay for medical reports. The fee should not be more than £75 each from your GP. New employer references will also be needed for you both and other references revisited as a significant time has elapsed. No reference was provided from David's first wife, so I am recommending that this also be revisited. The support network Eco Map will need to be redrawn bearing in mind the bereavement in David's family since the process began.

When all of these steps have been completed, a new report will need to be drafted. After that there will be an opportunity to attend another panel meeting, subject to satisfactory completion of these additional enquiries and availability of panel dates.

Please accept my assurances that your file and anything that has been discussed in relation to your application are confidential. All the members of the panel and your social worker are fully trained in data protection. Full details of the Council's data protection policy can be found on the website.

May I take this opportunity to thank you for the interest you have shown in fostering and adoption and wish you success in resolving your difficulties and with your future.

Yours sincerely,

Barbara Townsend
Agency Decision Maker

14.0 Post-Approval and Matching

Once the Agency Decision Maker has sent a letter confirming your approval, your social worker will be in touch to work with you on a matching plan (subject to a positive recommendation) and to advise on how best you will stay in contact with each other and the process for potential matches.

If there is a potential match, the allocated social worker will contact you either by phone or by email with details of the child. If everyone agrees that there may be a suitable match, you will be shown the child's profile and full history. The child's social worker will also be contacted.

If a match is agreed, we will arrange an initial meeting with the child's social worker, and if everything goes well you will be able to begin work on creating a bridging plan.

You are reminded that you will need to be available full-time for the minimum two-week bridging period. Both prospective adopters will need to be available for the bridging period if you are applying as a couple.

Further information about adoption leave and paternity leave is available on the Council's website and on the UK government website.

We hope you have found the journey to approval an educational one, and that you can now look forward to extending your family and providing a loving home for an adopted child!

DCYA/ PAW/socialservices/adoptionfostering/
adopterapproval/newversion5A/jan2011

The Baby Book

Hello. Have you come up to get away from it all, too? Bit noisy with all my nephews and nieces. Everyone's been so generous; we didn't expect presents. The new place is much smaller. Can you believe we've lived here for twelve years? Buying this house was the best thing we ever did, but we don't need all this space now.

Hey, let me show you this. I found it when we were packing. Bit dusty. It's the baby book she made for... for when we were trying to...

Of course, even when Cici was a kid in China everyone knew Winnie the Pooh. And I grew up on Christopher Robin. We'd decided that the nursery would be yellows and greens, nice spring colours to go with the garden. We were going to use those Disney stickers.

She did the design and chose all the images, but I persuaded her to put that one on the front. That's my favourite picture, 'cause we always imagined going down to the bridge and playing Pooh sticks. You can see the river from here. The new place is near a park too, so the dog will be happy. She loves that dog. Stupid name though.

The quotes are all from the original AA Milne books. Listen, 'Pooh, Piglet and Christopher Robin stood on the bridge watching the water, feeling the warm breeze that carried the smell of wild flowers.'

She fiddled with that ribbon for ages. It makes it special, you keep it fastened. They call it a Life Story Album, so when you adopt a child they can keep some memory of their birth family, maybe a photo or something from when they were born.

Then afterwards you add in pictures of the adopted family – me and Cici, and the kid's early childhood.

Each section has a different Pooh story. The idea is, we would put pictures of us in the album, holiday snaps, and you leave that with the foster carers, so when the baby meets you they know who you are. It opens up like this, you unfold that. It's held together by tiny magnets. So in here you put, say, a few wedding photos.

When I say 'baby', they're usually eighteen months to two years by the time they're adopted.

Kanga was the only female character, did you know that?

Always a girl, Cici was sure of that. We said officially we'd consider either gender, but she had dreams about all the girly things they would do together, and I'd already raised Danny.

Look at Christopher Robin and Piglet holding hands. You see, you'd slot your kid's picture in there at the back next to the tree.

And there was the other thing too – with me being older. The plan was that the daughter would grow up and be there for Cici when she's old. If we had... if it had happened, I'd have been seventy by the time she grew up.

See? There's a little tab there behind that honey pot. She made all the flowers individually by hand. She always talked about making things with a daughter.

It seemed like it was all we ever did together: hospitals and adoption procedures. The council were bloody invasive about Cici's treatment, amongst other things. You wouldn't believe how far back they go.

She was planning to have all the old pictures of her in this part, said Piglet was the cutest. I've got some great photos – Paris, Sorrento, Prague, Singapore. She'll have to make a different album now.

When this job came up we decided it was time to move on. It's a top university, and Cici's looking forward to her new job too.

They'll never admit it, but as long as they knew we were trying to start a family she was never going to get through the glass ceiling, even if she was smarter than any of them.

Look, this is a double section, so you could put three pictures on each side. That's the story of the woozle. Do you know that one? Pooh and Piglet follow the footprints of a mysterious creature, going round in circles till they realise they're following their own footsteps.

They wrote and said they wanted to do a whole load more investigations and we effectively had to start again. Neither of us could face going through all the assessments a second time. I got her the dog to cheer her up.

You like Tigger? He was Danny's favourite when he was little. This is the section for day trips to the seaside, parks, zoos.

I got a text from Danny at New Year. He's doing fine, met a girl, rows for the university. He couldn't make it today. It is a long way to come. I always say we should go to a match sometime, but he's at that stage in his life. She's making an album for Danny's twenty-first. I've got great pictures of him up trees and at Llandudno and Conway Castle. I'd have liked to have done it all again for Cici.

She painted the honey pots on herself and all those bees; took her ages. Cici always fancied keeping bees. Clive next door keeps them, said he'd set us up with all the gear. But she'd have had me in the mask, dealing with it all. Besides, it wouldn't have been practical with a child. We can do more outdoor things now.

This section would be for school. First day at school, class photo, sports day, school trips, that sort of thing. That's why it's got Christopher Robin with his books. It's really clever how it unfolds. There's space for about eight pictures in this section.

I never really knew the story about Owl. Wise, I suppose? We were going to put our graduation pictures in there. Cici used to do about three hours' homework every night for her accounting qualifications. The social worker told us not to use those pictures in our profile – she said it would put the children's social workers off. But this was our album, they couldn't tell us what to do.

After she finished studying, she had time for creative things like this. She designs amazing hand-made birthday cards. She makes one every birthday for all the nephews and nieces. They can all come and see us in the country.

Oh, in case I forget, do you know anyone that wants any baby stuff? My sisters all kept bringing round stair gates and car seats, and there's a cot in the nurse– … in there, from James, my Godson. Most of it's nearly new. I need to sort it all out. There are two sofas downstairs we're not keeping. It's the right thing though. We don't need this big house for two of us.

Eeyore was my favourite. I had a toy one and the tail was meant to come off. I lost it when I was eleven and never found it again.

Do you want another drink? I think I'm supposed to circulate but I'd rather stay up here for a bit. I'd better fasten it up again, tie the ribbon. She would have been a good mum, Cici. She's the only one that ever looked after me.

And that white space is where you put the name. You don't get to choose the name when you adopt. Talking of names, I'd better take that daft dog out in a minute.

No, I'm not hungry. I'll wait till everyone's gone. There'll be loads left over.

She'll be pleased you like the album.

Thanks for coming.

Author's Note

This is a work of fiction, and it is worth stating clearly that the people and events are made up. The various application forms and adoption procedures described do not reflect the precise processes or documents employed by any single organisation, but every attempt has been made to be authentic in general. This means that if the fictional characters are asked for lists of past relationships or safety details, those are the sorts of things that are likely to be required in any real adoption process. Certain liberties have been taken with the sequence and wording of the official forms, partly to avoid the perception of any real document being copied and also to suit the flow and contents of the fiction.

Information about the real processes is readily available from a number of sources, including CoramBAAF, an independent adoption and fostering organisation. Adoption has brought happiness and safety to many thousands of children and their adopted families. This book should not deter any individual who might provide a home for a child in care from considering adoption. There are presently over 70,000 children in care in the UK. Grateful thanks is given for the dedication of social workers, foster carers and many others involved in the processes of adoption and fostering.

Acknowledgements

My thanks to:

Sara Hunt and all at Saraband, especially Aisling Holling and Rosie Hilton, for believing in *Approval* and making some words into a book. Craig Hillsley for astute editing. Daniel Gray for wonderful design. Sarah S for the sense check.

Rodge Glass, my official lifelong mentor, for his patience and insight. Kim Wiltshire, without whom the concept of this book would not have come about. Ailsa Cox for balancing personal kindness with objective advice on the work. All the many members of NRG past and present for support and inspiration.

The lecturers and writers at Lancaster University for teaching me to write, in particular Jenn Ashworth, Paul Farley, George Green, Zoe Lambert and Graham Mort. The rest of The Band for friendship and advice over the last decade. Members of The Word group for the same.

Chris Forde at Preston's College for encouraging me to take writing seriously.

Lin for everything.

* * *

Versions of some of the chapters have been previously published as short stories; the publishers are gratefully acknowledged:

'Green Gables' was first published in *Unthology 5*, Unthank Books (2014)

'B' was first published in *Unthology 7*, Unthank Books (2015)

'David's Thing' was published in *An Earthless Melting Pot*, Quinn Publications (2015)

'Motivation' appeared in *7 Fictions, an anthology* by Edge Hill
  Associates that was distributed at the Cheltenham Literature
  Festival (2015)
'My Knee' was published in *Unthology 9*, Unthank Books (2017)
'Veritas Nunquam Perit, Part 1: The Last Sister' is available in text
  and audio on the MacGuffin platform run by Comma Press.
'Opposite Sides' was first published in *The Wall*, an anthology by the
  Institute for Creative Enterprise at Edge Hill University (2019)
'Veritas Nunquam Perit, Part II: Our Lady's Toes' was first published
  in the *Journal of the Short Story in English* (2019)
'Her Shoes' was first published in *3 Moon Magazine* (2020)

Dr John D Rutter teaches, edits, studies and writes short stories.
He has lectured at Edge Hill University, UCLan and for Comma
Press. His stories have been published as chapbooks, as well as in
various anthologies and newspapers and on websites. *Approval* is
his first book and was the winner of the NorthBound Book Award
2020. John lives in Preston, Lancashire, with his wife, Lin Zhang.
They have no children.

The NorthBound Book Award was created in 2019 to celebrate
the richness of writing from the North of England and the inno-
vative spirit of independent publishing. It is managed as part of
the Northern Writers' Awards. The 2020 award was supported
by New Writing North, as part of the Northern Writers' Awards,
and Saraband. New Writing North are an Arts Council National
Portfolio Organisation.